DO NOT PLAY MY
VIDEO GAME

Look for More Terrorlands Books
by Marco Chu Kwan Ching

TERRORLAND

Do Not Play My Video Game

MARCO CHU KWAN CHING

A
PEAR
PAPERBACK

Cover image © Dusan Kostic | Dreamstime.com (Royalty - Free License)

ISBN: 978-0-6482760-7-4

First printing in 2017
Second printing in 2019

PART 1

1

The high wall of Lorthic castle loomed into sight as I ascended the rugged slope of the stretched stone stairway. Tall, weathered castle walls rose high above the dreadful lemon sky.

Here I am. I have finally reached Lorthic.

When I looked back, I could see nothing but snow and sky.

I must pass Ciema's dire message back to King Lorthic and warn him about the coming threat our kingdom is about to face.

The storm delayed me.

My body was exhausted after pressing on for days. My toes and fingers felt numb.

Snow trickled down my face. The cold burned my skin. Even in a full suit of armor, I could still feel the crystal cold damp air wrapped around my freezing body.

The snow turned heavier. I could see nothing but layers of thick snowdrifts piled against the balusters and decayed stonewall.

Slowly, cautiously, I walked up the stairs.

Sheets of ice blanketed my every step and slowed my pace.

Gusts of strong merciless wind made my whole body shiver.

*Just take a small nap … you have done quite enough …
now have your rest...*

A soft accursed voice whispered in my ears.

Who is that?

I was too weak to find out now … too weak … too tired …

I staggered my way up the stairs as everything turned zig-zag.

I was losing my consciousness.

Slowly, I knelt.

My whole body was fatigued.

The sound of the howling wind was getting louder and louder as if it was trying to devour my consciousness.

And then I was absorbed in the thoughts of the accursed voice once again.

*Yes… you have done quite enough … the fire fades …
the mantle of the Lord interests you none … for that is your
curse … you can now rest in peace.*

My mind was clouded by dreadful thoughts.

When the snow cleared a little, what appeared in front of my eyes horrified me.

Oh no … I … I am too late … I am too late …

I saw rains of arrows pierced through the silver armor of the fallen Lorthic knights. Their bodies stood still and lifeless. Beneath my feet were crumbling cracked rocks layered on top of each other, caked with moss and dried blood. The once proud Lorthic's banner had collapsed.

It is all over ... I am too late ...

I felt defeated.

As I collapsed onto the ground in despair, a mysterious ring landed onto the pile of snow in front of me.

The golden flickering edge of the ring was somewhat familiar.

I realized it was no ordinary ring.

It is the Covetous Gold Serpent Ring – a gift of faith from the High Elves to the Lord of Lorthic for their alliance. The inscription on the ring was in Elvish letters. Rumors once said that the golden serpent would come alive and hiss when its ring-bearer was facing danger.

As I reached out to touch the ring, a vision struck my mind like an electric shock.

The next moment I found myself lying down on a peaceful garden. I could hear the sound of the birds. Evergreen leaves blanketed my whole body. Shimmering sunlight escaped from the gap of the leaves.

I am no longer in the snow.

I felt warm and alive once again.

Standing in front of me was a tall lady of extraordinary beauty and dressed in purest white. She had silk like skin. Her long river of hair shone the golden color of the sun. Beautiful, sparkling wisps were dancing around her. As she approached me, the aura of her lordliness radiated.

"Your Royal Highness," I said and knelt respectfully.

"I know who you are. I am the guardian of the Golden Wood. Few have spoken my name. Lorthic has fallen ... the covenant between men and elves is broken ... the fire fades..."

I followed behind the lady as she guided me to the inner part of the garden.

Up ahead, I saw a spectacular silvery mirror dish.

It was filled with water.

A parrot with vibrant color landed beside the mirror. It was studying me with suspicious eyes.

"Come." The lady motioned me over to look into the mirror. "Let the mirror guide your way."

As I stepped forward, the clashing sound of my armor scared the parrot away.

The lady took her flask and slowly poured water onto the mirror.

I lowered my head and glimpsed.

Everything looked so clear, so real. My reflection clearly revealed that I had aged.

The sound of the pouring water continued.

Slowly, my reflection distorted.

The ripples soon blended the vision of the mirror into something...

Something different ...

My eyes opened wide.

I could no longer see myself but terror approaching.

I heard screams.

I saw destructions.

I saw the kingdom of Lorthic was under siege. And villages, one by one, were burning in flames.

I saw the innocents fleeing helplessly and the lords surrendering their thrones.

The magnificent statue of Lorthic crumbled into ashes.

Oh wait. It was Irina, a daughter in the royal family of Lorthic! She was held captive and guarded by scythe-wielding wraiths.

My heart was pounding fast as I saw my once-peaceful homeland in flames.

Next, I saw an unfathomably powerful demon whose body was a combination of fire and ice crystals. This frightening destroyer infiltrated the High Wall of Lorthic Castle unchallenged.

The inferno from the demon made me force myself to step back from the mirror.

My Covetous Gold Serpent Ring was burning hot. The serpent on the ring hissed.

Suddenly, everything surrounding me began to fade.

"Lorthic has fallen … the covenant is broken … the fire fades … Prince Lorthic is in your hands … Please … save his soul. Tell him he …"

The lady's musical voice faded as my subconscious returned to my body.

I founded myself in front of the High wall of Lorthic once again.

The snow melted as the sun rose from the mountain ridges.

Maybe there was still hope.

The Lorthic gateway was just up ahead – wide opened. There was no time to waste.

I had to hurry.

Just as my faith was about to restore, the ground trembled and made me stagger.

Before I could regain my balance, the sky was casting a long stretched shadow where I stood. A strong gust of wind from behind pushed me forward.

Large chunk of rocks collapsed from the high wall of Lorthic castle. Small fragments scattered as I dodged.

I looked up and my eyes opened wide in shock.

My eyes met those of the creature.

The creature's intense eyes were lamp-like orange. Wisp of smoke breathing from its nostrils melted the surrounding snow. Its scales glistened and flittered in the sunlight as it spread its huge bat-like wings.

It is a wyvern.

With an angry growl, it shifted its gaze and flew in my direction.

A sharp cry escaped my mouth.

The next thing I saw was black.

2

"What are you two doing in the middle of the night?"

A thundering voice from nowhere made Mike and I jump.

Huh? What is happening? I continued to press the controller but the TV was completely black.

Strong light blinded us as the light switched on.

"Tom and Mike! What time is it now?" Mom stood with arms akimbo, frowning at us in pajamas.

Dad was shaking his head. Disappointed.

Mike glanced at his iWatch.

It was showing one o' clock in the morning.

"Do you know the two of you need to go to school tomorrow?" Mom scolded.

"But mom, please let us pass this stage, please give us another fifteen minutes," Mike pleaded.

This was obviously not a good move. I had tried this before.

"Maybe just give them another fifteen minutes," Dad said, trying to help.

This is bad … very bad.

"Antonio, if you had not bought your kids this machine, they would have been in bed two hours ago. Tom's grade has been dropping since the last semester when you bought them this thing. He cannot concentrate on the schoolwork. And next year, if his grade is not good enough, he is not going to a selective high school," Mom replied sharply.

"But I'm not the one who is going to high school next year," Mike protested.

Why did Mike have to be so stupid all the time? He was throwing gasoline on the fire.

I closed my eyes, praying mom did not know how to turn off the machine.

But she did.

***

In the morning, I was yawning all my way to school.

Noel tapped my back from behind. "Tom, you looked like you didn't sleep the whole night. What are you up to?"

Like me, Noel is a gamer - a real professional gamer. We have been best friends for nine years. We know just about everything about each other. For instance, I know that Noel still wore that Starcraft Protoss T-shirt he ordered from the Blizzard website.

You should have seen his fingers dance around on the keyboard as if he was a performance grade piano player. Sometimes, I thought he should go to Korea. Starcraft was a sport over there.

"Yo, wait up you two," a voice boomed from behind, which almost reminded me of Treebeard in The Lord of the Rings.

Of course I didn't have to turn around to find out it was Isaac. He is the only one in school to have such a strange voice.

I turned around and saw Isaac's dopey grin. Isaac was quite tall and obese for his age. Even though we were twelve, Isaac towered over us like someone from Year 10. His tall figure blocked us from the sunlight, which was wonderful. That is why Isaac had the nickname of Tree-beard.

"What have you guys got for the rest of the week?" Isaac asked.

"I have neither tests nor assignments. I have nothing. I'm totally free for the rest of the week," Noel said.

"Me too," I joined.

"Do you know the creator of the Dark Legend series is coming to attend a launch event in San Francisco?" Isaac asked.

"Do you mean Hidetaki Kojima?" I exclaimed.

Hidetaki Kojima was my hero. He was a pure genius. His Dark Legend series was incredible and I thought about it even in my sleep.

It was punishing, replayable and challenging.

It had a very steep learning curve.

Every element of the game had an immense weight to it.

Every skirmish had a different situation that could seriously affect your tactics.

Every enemy demand could not be underestimated.

Every attack and dodge could be the difference between life and death for both the player and enemy.

"You gotta be kidding me?" Noel said, shaking his head in disbelief.

"We grew up with this medieval RPG series. I still remember how the three of us slept over in Issac's house, trying to beat the Devourer of Angels in Dark Legend One." I tried to recall the memory.

"Big bosses! I love big bosses." Noel smiled.

"So, when is Hidetaki Kojima coming?" I asked.

"Well, he is coming this Saturday. The launch event will be held at 8:00am inside the entertainment center. Rumors say that Hidetaki Kojima will be releasing a new title in the Dark Legend series."

3

Issac, Noel and I arrived at the entertainment center an hour before the admission and it was filled with people.

Queues of people were lining up next to the rows of flags on both sides.

The flags were printed with game titles familiar to kids of our age.

Some staff were dressed in cosplay as featured characters in video games. Some die-hard fans were shouting slogans. And the rest of them were busy making friends with one another, discussing their favorite video games to be launched.

To be honest with you, we were pretty excited and proud of ourselves getting up so early on a Saturday morning.

This had never happened before in our history.

So, what was behind our drive?

We were just feeling ecstatic.

We never thought we would be able to meet Hidetaki Kojima in person and learn about his new game.

Not this soon. Not this close. Not like this.

We could finally see the entrance in the distance as we

followed the snake-like queue and edged forward slowly on the red-cobbled street.

Faint music could be heard behind the tall entrance.

"Hidetaki Kojima has an ocean of fans," Isaac exclaimed.

"Well, not that many in U.S. actually, you should have a look at what happened in Tokyo," Noel suggested.

"The last Dark Legend sequel earned Kojima a remarkable reputation. The game itself was rated as the game of the year by IGN," I added.

"And it was so good that we have not even finished it," Isaac mocked.

"Well, the game is designed to be punishing," I defended.

"If you feel aggravated, you should go and play Super Mario," Noel teased.

"Hey mate, the old Dark Legend is nothing compared to what you are about to see." A big guy interrupted us from the back. "Hidetaki Kojima wants to take the gamers' experience to the next level and he made a special piece of hardware just for it."

"Huh? What hardware?" Our mouths dropped open. We thought we were big fans. This guy seemed to know more than us.

"The new Dark Legend game that you will see later is played with a specially made virtual reality headset. It is an entirely different experience," the big guy said excitedly.

What did he mean by a specially made virtual reality headset?

Just before the big guy could leak any more information, the front door of the entertainment center burst open.

Everyone's attention turned to the entrance as a cold breeze of air swept over us. Dozens of staff hurried out and welcomed us with their warming smile. We went through the ticket booth and entered the interior of the entertainment center. The rap music ramped up so loud inside that we couldn't hear one another.

"Hey!" Isaac finally gave up on calling us as he tapped his hands on our shoulders. "Look over there!"

We followed his gaze and saw rows of 42" TV screens connected to Wii, XBOX ONE and PS4, aligned neatly with one another. Different stands were advertising games that are going to be launched this year.

A few booth babes smiled and waved a welcome gesture at us.

Big advertising boards were showcasing Battlefield X and Minecraft.

Sonic the Hedgehog walked past us clumsily and stirred up a wave of excitement.

We made a few turns and stopped by to look at the new titles.

"God, this is awesome!" Noel's eyes were filled with passion.

It was the blockbuster shooting game called Call of Duty.

Seriously, I think it was legendary. This franchise's cinematic, immersive storytelling style, and all the explosions were absolutely engaging.

Like Noel, I was also a big fan of shooting games. I played Doom, Halo, Gears of War and Battlefield 4.

My brother and I played them in cooperation mode every Friday night.

Just when I was about to call Isaac to come over, I saw him looking at the LEGO Worlds. It was hilarious to see Isaac, with the size of an adult, filled with joy when he picked up games like this.

Anyway, even though we loved different genres of game, one game we commonly loved and hated was Dark Legend. I don't know what kind of magic it had on us. We cracked at least two controllers because of the frustrations throughout the game.

Usually gamers do not stick around and stay engaged with highly difficult games. What makes this one different is that it has a very steep, brutal leaning curve.

We turned a few corners and arrived at the center of the entertainment center. It was like a large conference room with a big TV screen on the stage.

Everyone was seated.

Suddenly, an announcement interrupted my thoughts.

A voice echoed around the room. "Next, we are delighted and privileged to have the opportunity to invite Kojima san all the way from Japan to talk about his upcoming game: Dark Legend – Scholar of the Abyss."

The next moment we saw an Asian man hurry up to the stage with enthusiasm.

The Asian guy looked skinny. He had narrowed eyes behind those J.R. Rey frames. His black hair covered most of his forehead. He waved to us as he hurried up to the stage.

"Hello everyone," he said in Japanese and the crowd cheered.

It was Hidetaki Kojima.

I couldn't believe my own eyes. I saw him! The creator of my beloved Dark Legend sequel!

I couldn't help but join the rest of the crowd of fans.

Camera flashes were everywhere.

I sent a picture of Kojima san to my sleeping brother just to make him envy me.

Kojima san's wrinkles spread across his face when he smiled.

As soon as he spoke, the cheers and yells of the crowd died down.

"This is my 31st year in the game industry. I have visited many studios around the world, meeting many great people. Over the years, we were looking for a realistic presentation of our games. We really want to make something that is different. Something that is out-of-the-box. I came up with several ideas. Sometimes people have an idea from when they were a child, and they'll turn that into a game when they're an adult. But that is not the way we approach the subject because the gaming industry is always evolving. And the Dark Legend sequel was to answer to that. But to take gaming experience to another level, I am looking for a very photo-realistic presentation, I want gamers to get a feel and sense of the environment. For that reason, we need special hardware. That is why we partnered up with Forever Studio. They handed over what was basically the crystallization of their efforts over many years," Kojima san explained in his Japanese accent.

The crowd went completely silent as they listened to their idol continue with his presentation.

What was the hardware that Kojima san was talking about?

"Who has played Dark Legend?" Kojima san finally asked the crowd.

Everyone put up their hands.

"Anyone who has played my games will know that they are rather stressful games, where you have to play for a long time," Kojima san replied.

Everyone laughed in agreement.

"As a game creator, I'm not one hundred percent satisfied when looking back at the previous game that I released. And that is why I created Dark Legend – Scholar of the Abyss." Kojima san smiled.

The light above our heads got dimmer and dimmer.

The next thing we saw was the red velvet curtain parting behind Kojima san.

Then everything went dark.

"Now, I want all of you to look for a device beneath your seat and put it on." Kojima san echoed in darkness.

What was Kojima san talking about?

"What is going on?" I heard Isaac whispering in the darkness.

It seemed that he was as puzzled as me.

"Found it," Noel said as he helped us to locate it too.

Although I couldn't see the device in the darkness, I could feel it was a headset. And it seemed to be wireless. The unit was light as feather. Even when I wore glasses, I felt quite natural and comfortable.

We followed Kojima san's instruction to turn it on.

There was a slight pressure at the back of my head, but it was soon alleviated.

I pressed the ON button and waited.

Nothing happened.

"Hey, Noel, do you see anything?" I asked.

No reply.

All of a sudden, I felt a sudden breeze that made my whole body shiver.

Wow. What was going on? It is freezing cold.

Howling wind began to blow against my face.

Kojima san's voice became distant and slowly overwhelmed by the sound of the wind.

"Isaac?" I tried to reach out for my friend in darkness but I could feel nothing but thin air.

Wow. What was going on?

All of a sudden, I felt like I was lost in another dimension.

The howling wind rang in my ears.

Snowflakes blew into my face.

I lowered my head and trudged down the road towards the Antarial Keep.

Even though the keep was just up the hill, everything seemed miles away as I walked into the blowing snow.

I squinted through the sheet of white falling snow and saw the steeple of ice tower.

Even from below, the windows of the tower glared into mine like evil back eyes.

This ice tower must be where Antarial hid, I decided.

This Maiden of Anguish must be what the villagers are talking about.

> *When the snow blows wild*
> *And doomsday comes close,*
> *Beware, Antarial, adventurers*
> *Beware, Antarial,*
> *She brings the cold*

The rhyme returned to me through the whisper of the wind.

A couple of centuries ago, there was a rumor in this humble, small town of Kukri. An ancient evil was slayed by a group of heroes and its soul was trapped within a magic moonstone beneath the Monastery of Kukri. The heroes warned the village to guard the Monastery, and ordered no one to ever go inside.

Over the course of many generations, something that should not have been forgotten was lost.

Soon, history became legend.

Legend became myths.

Myths became rumors.

Soon, the King of Lorthic established himself as a king and made Kukri his capital city. The ancient monastery became his cathedral.

Over time, villages were formed in the surrounding area of Kukri.

But the rumors of Kukri did not die away.

After listening to rumored riches within the cathedral, King Lorthic ordered his most trusted lieutenant, Antarial, and his elite army to venture deep inside the cathedral.

However, they did not return.

Some rumors said they escaped the kingdom with the treasures they sought. Others said they were abandoned when they attempted to call the King for help.

Either way, ever since Antarial and the elite guards disappeared, everyone agreed that strange moans were heard from within the cathedral.

King Lorthic had forbidden everyone from talking about this tragedy.

Soon after, Kukri was attacked by a horde of demons.

The once-holy cathedral became a hideous place filled with dark cults and rituals.

This attracted many adventurers to come and find out what happened.

I was one of them.

I pulled back my hood on and staggered up the hill.

The blizzard was abnormally strong.

The weather pushed me back, and forced me to turn around every step I made.

"Does it ever stop snowing here?" I grumbled.

My intuition was telling me there was some kind of dark magic manipulating the weather.

I pressed on and headed up the winding hill path.

My scream caught in my throat when one of my boots accidentally slipped into the thick, wet snow.

Then I realized there were footsteps.

I wondered who could that be?

I picked up my pace and followed the track.

More footsteps magically appeared in front of me.

Strange.

Soon, I arrived in front of a snow hut where the roof-top was blanketed with sheets of white snow. Dim yellow light from a lantern illuminated the entrance. Dark smoke was rising from the chimney on top of the roof. Behind the hut was an infinite field of palm trees in the snow.

I staggered my way to the snow hut.

The wooden floor creaked beneath the weight of my heavy sabatons.

Oops.

I wondered who would live in the middle of the snow mountain, far away from the village. Well, maybe I should take a rest inside and wait for the blizzard to die down a bit.

"Hello?" I knocked on the door.

No reply.

I peered inside the window and saw no one, but there were three heavy brass candlesticks on a wooden table.

Clearly, there must be inhabitants.

I tried the door one more time and burst in with my heavy armor.

I landed hard onto the ground.

Suddenly, I heard laughter.

Laugher?

I was confused for a while and then I heard applause.

Bright light blinded me from above when I took off my VR headset.

The next minute, I saw an Asian face smiling in front of me.

"Get up! What are you doing up there?" a familiar voice shouted from nowhere.

When I turned around, I saw Noel and Isaac laughing their heads off.

Oh no! This couldn't be happening …

Before I realized what happened, a pair of arms pulled me up from my knees.

The spotlight shone on me as if I was the focus of the crowd.

I was actually up on the stage with Kojima san!

How did that happen?

"This is the power of Forever Studio's VR hardware."

Kojima san spoke to the audience. "It is the future of gaming: movies and games will be merged into one."

Kojima san stopped and turned to me.

"So, our little friend, what is your name?" Kojima san asked, and handed his microphone to me.

"M…my name is Tom," I stammered.

I didn't usually feel embarrassed. But facing hundreds of people below did make me feel kind of nervous.

"Excellent Tom. Can you share with everyone what you just experienced?" Kojima san asked again.

I looked at the crowd and took a deep breath.

"Well, I felt as if I were inside the game myself. It was more than just a movie. I … I saw myself on a snow mountain. I felt so cold. Everything seemed so realistic. The sense … the graphics … the sound effects … every-thing was just too real that my mind actually made me believe I am the main character of the game!" I stam-mered.

I looked at the crowd. But it seemed that everyone was puzzled.

Even Isaac and Noel frowned.

Everyone looked at me from below as if I was from outer space.

Hello? Did I say something wrong?

I spun around and turned to Kojima san.

He tilted his glasses and studied me carefully.

"It seems that Dark Legend – Scholar of the Abyss has chosen you," Kojima san grinned.

"Huh? What is that supposed to mean?" I asked.

The entertainment center brightened and two staff members in uniform hurried up onto the stage with a gift box. They had the shiniest smile I have ever seen. The printing on the box was spectacular. The entire box was white in color. It was engraved with vintage medieval patterns. The eye-catching logo of Dark Legend – Scholar of the Abyss was embossed at the front. And the words "Collector's Edition" were evenly spaced on top of the box.

I was stunned.

Did you know Dark Legend – Scholar of the Abyss won't be released for several more months?

I was looking at a pre-released product of my dream.

"Congratulations Tom, this is a gift from me." Kojima san's grin went wider. "I'm afraid you will be the first person in the U.S. to experience the future of video games."

I was ecstatic.

I felt like I was the luckiest guy on the planet. Not only did I manage to see Kojima san in person, I was also interviewed by him and got a prize!

In the end, we took a photo together, which I am going to keep for eternity.

I am serious. Not many people had the chance to get this close to their idol. Not to mention the interaction we had.

Isaac and Noel will envy me for a very long time.

When the event finally ended, they helped me to carry the Dark Legend Collector's Edition all the way home.

It was quite heavy to be honest.

It made me wonder what was actually inside the box.

"So, what makes you so brave that you staggered all the way up onto the stage?" Noel asked me on our way back to my home.

"You don't believe me, do you?" I sounded a bit upset.

"Not until you tell us the whole story," Isaac said.

"I was not lying. Didn't you hear what Kojima san

said?" I protested.

"Yeah. He said the game has chosen you," Isaac said. "But, I think he is just being funny."

I shrugged.

My two suspicious friends looked at me as if I was some kind of alien from space.

"What?" I asked.

"Nothing, there must be something…." Noel frowned as he whispered to himself.

A while later, we were finally back in front of my house.

Ding Dong.

I pressed the doorbell. "Mom, Dad, I'm back! Isaac and Noel are coming over for a short visit."

No reply.

I pressed the doorbell a couple of times but it seemed no one was at home.

Strange. It was only two in the afternoon. Where could everyone be?

Mike had to be home. He was going to have tests next week. No way Mom would let him out this weekend.

"Are you telling us you don't have the key?" Noel sounded disappointed.

"You know we are not going to help you carry this game home without unboxing it with you," Isaac insisted.

"I know. I know." I uttered a sigh.

I pressed the doorbell continuously.

Suddenly, the door burst open.

It was my brother.

Goodness me. He was still in his pajamas! He yawned at us as he opened the door. His hair was all messy and his eyes looked weary.

"What's up?" Mike yawned.

"God! Are you telling me you just woke up?" I was a bit frustrated.

"Hmmm… of course not," Mike denied. "In fact, I got up earlier than you."

I rolled my eyes. "Yes. Like three in the morning and you went back to sleep at eight."

Mike giggled.

Isaac and Noel said hello to Mike as we came in.

"Where are Mom and Dad?" I asked my brother as we took our sneakers off.

Then I immediately went to the drawers to find some undersized slippers for my friends.

It is a rule not to wear sneakers in my house. Mom will not tolerate anyone walking around the house with sneakers on. I meant it.

Mike smiled. "Well… they won't be back tonight. They are going to catch up with Uncle Banana and spend one night at the resort."

"Your brother is funny. Who is this Uncle Banana?" Isaac said, and Noel burst out laughing.

"No. He meant Uncle Banara," I corrected my brother. "In fact, he is a game designer too."

Mike stared at my two friends in amazement when he saw them carrying a big box.

"Wow, what is that? Let me have a look. Let me have a look!" Mike cried in excitement.

"It's that new game you've been anticipating for the entire year."

I smiled as I walked to the kitchen to prepare some

drinks for my friends.

Isaac and Noel put the box on the floor and let Mike examine it.

"Are ... are you telling me you bought this? It looks spectacular," Mike stammered. "Bu ... but it's not going to be released until next month. So, how did you get this?"

"I didn't buy it. You haven't read my message, have you?" I asked.

"Did you send me anything?" Mike replied.

"This is a gift from the creator of Dark Legend." I felt a moment of pride when I said that.

"Stop making things up," Mike denied.

"I'm serious," I insisted.

My friends didn't reply. They gulped and finished the glass of apple juice I poured.

"Do you argue with your brother like this all the time?" Noel teased.

"You would know how it feels if you had a brother," I replied.

My brother flipped the box upside down and studied the description.

"Careful," I warned, worried stiff.

My brother ignored me and continued to read.

"I have been waiting for this moment for a long time." Isaac grinned, exposing his teeth.

"I wonder how much torture we will get for the rest of the day," Noel anticipated.

"So, I guess we won't be sleeping tonight, will we?" I smiled.

"Hey, guys, come and check this out." Mike gestured

us to come over just when I was about to show my friends upstairs.

"What's wrong? Please don't tell me you've broken it already." I peered down from halfway up the stairs.

"Why would I do something like that?" Mike dropped his mouth open.

When the three of us hurtled over to Mike to find out what was going on, our heart almost skipped a beat at what we saw.

"Wh…why do you unbox it?" I was horrified, and collapsed onto my feet.

My friends shook their head, disappointed.

"Well, I just want to see what was inside," Mike stammered, feeling guilty.

"It's okay, it was just a matter of time before we opened it anyway." Noel tried to comfort me.

I felt annoyed.

I stared at Mike in disgust. Why does he always have to ruin all the great moments? If you are not a gamer, you probably think I am fussy. But, unboxing a game is part of the overall gaming experience, especially for a magnificently designed game in special edition.

Oh well, there was not much point blaming Mike now.

"Tom, I found a strange message inside the box," Mike said, motioning me to look inside the box.

PLAYERS BEWARE
DO NOT PLAY MY VIDEO GAME

"That is Kojima san's humorous style of introducing the game. He wants to manipulate players to think the game is real." Noel chucked.

I looked at the warning sign.

Images of the game flashed in my mind like scattered memories.

I knew that this was just a game.

But what I experienced in the entertainment center was too real to be called a game. I could feel the cold, I could touch the objects, just like what I experienced in real life.

How did that happen?

"Hello. Anybody home?" Mike waved his hands in front of me and interrupted my thoughts.

"Are you okay?" Isaac worried. "You looked lost."

"Do you want to take a nap while the three of us have a head start?" Noel teased.

"I though you were going to turn into a wyvern like the one we saw last night and start breathing fire on me because I unboxed the game," Mike said.

"I am fine." I shook away my thoughts.

It was just a game. What else could it be? Was I right?

"My parents are seldom away from home. Today is the greatest opportunity in the history of mankind," I joked.

Mike nodded, eyes closed. "I totally agree."

The four of us went upstairs to my room.

I tried my best to clear the room up a bit so it didn't look too messy.

Mike immediately fired up the game console and set up the TV.

"You are helpful," I said sarcastically.

"This is called division of labor," my brother said to defend himself.

My two friends took everything out of the box.

Noel was reading the manual as if he was going to have exams, while Isaac was examining the hardware.

"Hey Tom, check this out." Isaac waved at me. "Kojima san gave you four VR headsets and four motion controllers. They looked different to those I saw back in the entertainment center. Th…they are incredibly light. Look at their shape. They look so futuristic."

"Impressive," Noel exclaimed.

"Four headsets with four motion controllers? Does that mean we can play together?" Mike guessed.

"But the previous Dark Legends games are only single player, right?" Isaac asked.

"Well, maybe they incorporate cooperative mode," I shrugged. "Who knows."

"How?" Mike frowned.

Mike loved asking questions. Silly questions. Trivial Questions. He loved to ask something that he already knew the answer to. I don't know why he behaved like this. Maybe he loved to get attention.

"Because we are playing in VR mode," I replied.

The four of us mounted the VR headset on after we loaded the game into the machine.

I felt a tiny pressure pressed against my head just like before but the discomfort soon disappeared.

I wondered if it was just me.

Everything went black for a second and then the screen transitioned to white.

A beautiful 3D logo indent, animated with particles,

revealed itself with a whoosh sound.

"Wow, it looks so 3D. I am loving VR already," Mike cried.

"I know. It is absolutely gorgeous. Just like in the movies," Isaac added.

It is the future of gaming; movies and games will be merged into one.

I recalled what Kojima san said. I couldn't agree more with what he said. Apparently, it was the way the gaming industry was heading. Movies and games were merging to become one type of entertainment. With all the magnificent cut scenes, playing a video game really made me feel like watching a movie in a virtual reality environment. It was beyond how we enjoy a game in a conventional way.

A few more titles flew by and the screen transitioned to the game menu.

The surround sound effect and passing air tricked my mind to feel as if the titles flew from behind me.

How can I describe it more precisely?

Well, if you have been to Movie World on the Gold Coast, you must have seen Warner Bros's Looney Tunes 4D Wile E. Coyote and Road Runner. Apart from seeing the 3D film, we also experienced physical effect in synchrony. We would feel effects like rain, wind, strobe lights and vibration.

"Wow, can you feel that?" Mike exclaimed. "Where does the air come from?"

"I have no idea. I fell in love with it even before the game has even begun," Isaac said.

"Really? I though you are a big fan of Nintendo games only," Noel teased.

The game menu had a video background of a ruined medieval town. A full moon, yellow as a lemon, floated high in the dark sky. Black clouds were drifting over it. In front of me, we saw colorful wisps flying by randomly. A dirty path stretched all the way to the town. The background music was a sad but beautiful female choir that made the environment kind of ghostly.

Game buttons revealed themselves in front of us with a fancy light streak transition.

"Cool," all of us exclaimed.

I pressed start.

I couldn't wait to see what happened next.

Just as all of us were expecting to transit into an in-game cut scene, the game menu halted.

"Huh? What is going on?" Mike sounded frustrated.

"Just be patient," I suggested.

We waited for another two minutes but the screen in our VR headset was just unresponsive!

"Is there something wrong with the disk?" Noel speculated.

"Strange. It should be brand new. I doubt there are scratches on it," I replied.

A moment later, we saw glitches and distorted noises through our VR screen.

"There is definitely something wrong with the disk," Mike concluded. "I am hoping to – "

Before Mike could finish, the four of us dropped our mouths open at what we saw.

W e saw breaking news from a Japanese TV channel with English subtitles!

The four of us were puzzled.

MASSIVE DISAPPEARANCE REPORTED AFTER PLAYING VIDEO GAMES

TOKYO DAILY, TD - Three more children were reported missing earlier this week, making Takuji Komatsu and Hiroshi Arikawa the ninth and tenth victims in the reign of mysterious disappearances that has been terrorized the city since mid-March this year.

Both victims, aged 12, were reported missing by concerned parents. Although the police department has issued no formal statement, parents of the victims reported that all their children had been to a Tokyo game show and played the newly released game called Dark Legend - Scholar of the Abyss. Whether or not this is just a coincidence has yet to be announced.

Hidetaki Kojima, the creator of the best selling game series, Dark Legend, gave a public speech in the U.S. today, saying he is confident that he will revolutionize the entire gaming industry. He denied the speculation about the game being related to the missing children.

Forever Studio, the partner of Hidetaki Kojima, come out today to clarify how their newly released game and the mysterious disappearance of children are two independent events. The company said they will cooperate with the police and hope the missing children return home safely.

"What is happening?"

"Can someone tell me what is going on?" Isaac sounded anxious.

"Mike, did you do something and change the channel?" I accused my brother.

"Tom, what is wrong with you. I didn't press anything. It seems that the news is part of the game content," Mike defended.

"Very funny, the news is from this week," I said sharply.

"Cut it out, the two of you," Noel said. " It seems that the news is really part of the game."

"That's impossible," I insisted.

Why would anyone in their right mind put content like this as part of the game? It didn't make any sense.

I really wanted to fast forward it but the control was unresponsive.

We were forced looked at the interview of the victim's parents.

Apparently, all of the parents reported that the last time they ever saw their children again was when they were playing the newly released Dark Legend game.

"Guys, this is getting creepy," Mike complained.

"Is that how Kojima san tries to blend movies and gaming together?" Noel laughed.

First, it was the message inside the box.

Now, it was this disturbing news.

I tried to piece the information together. My intuition told me that Kojima san didn't want people to play his game.

But that couldn't be right.

This was not the message Kojima san tried to deliver.

"Oh well, this is getting kind of boring. I'm out of here." Mike was fed up and began to take off the headset.

Suddenly, the screen glitched and the transition happened again.

Before we could realize what is happening, we were back to the medieval landscape again.

"Now, this is what I am talking about," Mike said, happy again.

We followed the bird's eye view and flew through the clouds, the medieval houses and the stables. Orange lantern light illuminated the door of every family.

The night was cold.

Lightning cut zig-zags into the dark sky, followed by a rumbling thunder.

Mike accidentally bumped into me and stepped on my foot.

"Ouch! Watch it!" I shrieked in pain.

"Sorry ... I am so sorry ...The lightning is ... so real. It ... it's going to rain," Mike complained.

Isaac and Noel giggled.

"Relax ... it's just virtual reality," I explained.

"But... it is so real," Mike continued.

"From now on, please keep a distance from one another," I suggested. "I don't want to end up in hospital after playing this game."

We all agreed.

A while later, a ruined stone monastery appeared in sight.

Even in a distance, I could barely see the dim flickering light inside the building.

Our camera flew through the window slowly.

Mysterious background music filled the atmosphere with suspense.

Then, we saw a medieval library filled with hundreds of wax dripping candles.

A beautiful girl in a red Corsair's overshirt was busy writing with her peacock feather pen. Her curly brown hair was smooth. Her ivory skin was silk-like. Her liquid brown eyes looked worried as she was summarizing text from a vintage book in front of her.

At some point, the tip of her feather pen broke, and ink scattered onto a spot of the page.

"None of these make any sense to me," she whispered to herself. "What am I missing?"

The fierce wind blew the window open and the pages of the vintage book flipped.

One of the flipping pages was showing the sketch of a magnificent castle overseeing surrounding towns. Another flipped page was showing the sign of a falling star.

The girl hurried to close the window before the rain showered the place.

A streak of bright lightning illuminated the library with a blinding flash of white.

When the wind finally stopped blowing, the girl returned back to her seat.

The vintage book was showing a giant lizard resting on the high wall of Lorthic.

Suddenly, the sound of a creaking door drew her attention to the library entrance.

"Who is that?" The girl grabbed a lantern from the table and pointed it to the source of the sound.

She wanted to know the history of the monastery, and that is why she was here.

Somehow, during her search, she accidentally stumbled into this medieval library.

Everyone knew the monastery was a forbidden place.

Legends say there were monsters lurking in the depth of the monastery. No one can explain the strange moans late at night.

Her intuition tells her something paranormal is going on.

Something evil was lurking in the monastery.

But the king turned a blind eye to that.

That is why she was out here at night, seeking evidence.

Step by step, she walked towards the entrance.

She pushed the door open slightly and the loud creaking sound of the wooden door sent a chill down her spine.

The dark corridor stretched to infinite abyss.

When she raised her lantern, she could barely see a few squeaky rats zigzagging left and right on the cold stone floor. They looked frightened.

The girl focused into the abyss for a long moment.

"Hello?" she asked.

Her voice echoed in the darkness of the corridor and then died away.

She took a few steps forward. She could hear nothing else but the sound of her breathing.

Well, maybe it was just an imagination.

Just as she was about to turn away, four amber-like eyes glowed in the dark, right in front of her!

The girl was frozen in terror.

The four of us uttered a shrill cry of fright as we were seeing everything as first-person view on our VR screen.

Tension swept all over our bodies as the creature revealed its gigantic head that filled the corridor.

Its face featured a large, glowing mouth full of dagger-like teeth and a forked tongue. Six insect-like legs lifted its torso and a long shadow cast over us.

"You thought you were so clever, that you had outwitted us all. One by one, our brethren fell into your trap, but not me. I defy you!" the monster snarled in rage.

The four of us took a step back without noticing.

The monster was so loud that we had no choice but to turn down the volume.

I kept on pressing the button but it didn't work!

The disgusting smell of the creature invaded our nostrils and made us feel sick.

"Turn it off!" Mike chocked.

"I am trying!" I said sharply.

"Try harder! It stinks!" Mike complained.

"What the – " Noel and Isaac were shocked. The VR headsets on our head became so incredibly tight that we couldn't take them off.

"Soon, my army will invade Lorthic castle, and ravage whoever seeks to bring hope of resistance," the creature continued.

"The power! Cut the power!" Noel suggested.

Just as I hurried to the power socket, the creature

reached out its reptilian hands and pulled all of us closer to it!

"Im ... impossible," Mike said, astonished.

We tried to scream but no sound came out.

The creature's grasp was so tight that it was impossible for us to resist.

Slowly, we were being lifted further and further away from the ground.

"Nooooooo!" we cried helplessly as the VR headset on our heads slowly disappeared.

"Let the game begin."

The creature dropped us into its mouth and began to feed.

PART 2

9

Just when we thought we were doomed, something else drew the creature's attention.

Blinding rays of orange-yellow slowly illuminated the dark corridor of the monastery.

Steam was rising from the supposed cold stone floor.

Hundreds, if not thousands, of rats swarmed out from the abyss.

Then the monastery began to shake.

Dust and debris collapsed from the wall and ceiling.

"Not…not again!" the creature cried in horror as it decided to flee.

The four of us collapsed onto the burning stone floor.

"Hot! Hot!" the four of us were dancing like chickens.

Before we realized what was happening, the girl in the red Corsair's Overshirt screamed at the top of her lungs.

"Duck!" she shrieked.

Everything happened so quickly; the next thing we heard was a loud collision.

And everything went black.

***

By the time I regained conscious, I found myself lying flat on the snow.

Howling wind was blowing fiercely against my body.

My fingers felt numb, because I had been in the cold for so long.

Everything looked too bright. I have to wait for my eyes to adjust the white glare of the snow.

I felt heavier than usual when I tried to lift my arm.

When I lowered my head, I saw myself suit up in shiny knight armor and gauntlets.

Huh? What is going on?

Slowly, I tried my best to get back up on my feet.

I spun around and found out that I was alone.

Everything else was buried under a thick sheet of snow that stretched for miles.

"Mike! Isaac! Noel! Where are you?" My voice came out weak.

No reply.

What is happening to me? Where is everyone? Why am I the only one here?

I walked aimlessly against the whistling wind.

Snowflakes fell on my knight helmet.

I staggered aimless, lost.

I tried to recall what happened, but my mind went blank.

The steeple of an ice tower above up ahead. The tower glared like evil black eyes.

I vaguely remembered I had been here before.

But, when was that?

I continued up the hill, but the weather pushed me

back, forced me to turn around every step I made.

I pressed on and headed up the winding hill path.

My scream caught in my throat when one of my boots accidentally slipped into the thick, wet snow.

Then I realized there were footsteps.

I wonder who could that be?

I picked up my pace and followed the track.

More footsteps magically appeared in front of me.

Soon, I arrived in front of a snow hut, where the rooftop was blanketed with sheets of white snow. Dim yellow light from a lantern illuminated the entrance. Dark smoke was rising from the chimney on top of the roof. Behind the hut was an infinite field of palm trees in the snow.

I staggered my way to the snow hut.

The wooden floor creaked beneath the weight of my heavy sabatons.

The creaking sound was like a flashback to me. I remembered this place. I remembered everything!

I am inside the game again!

Nooooooooooooo.

How do I get back to my world, this time, without the VR headset?

But, there is no point in panicking now.

Maybe I should take a rest inside the snow hut and wait for the blizzard to die down a bit.

"Hello?" I knocked on the door.

No reply.

I wondered who would live in the middle of the snow mountain.

I peered inside the window and saw no one, but there

were three heavy brass candlesticks on a wooden table.

Clearly, there must be inhabitants.

I tried the door one more time and burst in with my heavy armor.

I found myself in a warm kitchen. Light from the lantern on the ceiling flickered over the wall. Lumber-piles were stacked next to a wall-mounted wood-burning stove.

There was a wooden bowl with hot chicken soup on the wooden table, next to the candlesticks.

I raised the wooden bowl to my mouth, blew on it for a few second, and swallowed a mouthful.

Delicious.

The chicken soup soothed my dry, cold throat.

Just before I decided to take a few more spoonfuls, a weak, low moaning sound inside the house interrupted me.

"Who is that?" I asked.

I followed the trace of the sound.

The sound of my sabatons thundered every step I made.

Soon, I arrived in a room upstairs.

To my surprise, I saw a wounded warrior in a velvet blue cloak and green-gold like armor. A few arrows imbedded in this chest. I could barely see his face, as he was hooded. Next to him was a large silver dog grieving, lowering its head, and wagging its furry white tail.

Just as I wanted to walk in and help, the silver dog turned around and barked ferociously at me, jaws opened. Its round, blue eyes locked on me suspiciously.

"Silver, don't," the wounded warrior spoke weakly.

The dog stepped aside as soon as its master ordered it, but its eyes still locked on me as if I were a threat.

I looked at the wounded warrior as he clenched his teeth to resist the pain.

"Is there anything I can do? Are there any Chirurgeons around?" I tried to offer my help.

"Don't bother." The warrior unhooded himself and revealed his pointed ears. His long, golden-hair glinted like gold.

"Yo-you are an elf." I was astonished.

"My name is Quenya, the lieutenant of the Golden Wood. My army was supposed to be the reinforcement of King Lorthic to defend the invasion of the Hellspawn, led by Beelzebub," Quenya said, covering his wounds in pain.

"Where is the rest of your army?" I asked.

"We were ambushed by a horde of demons, led by Antarial. My army tried to fought off the demons before they reached the village of Kukur. But we were outnumbered," Quenya said, his gasp quickened.

"Wow...Relax...how can I save you?" I sounded worried.

It looked like the elf would pass away any moment.

"It...it is too late. I...I am dying. You cannot save me. Please...take this...take Anglachel back to the Guardian of the Golden Wood. Let her know what happened." Quenya gasped as he handed me a sheathed sword.

"What is this about?" I tried to reject his offer, but Quenya insisted to pass his sword to me.

"Please tell the Guardian I am sorry. I should have lis...listened to her warning. This accursed blade should be silence. She is right about -" Quenya closed his eyes before he could finish.

His limbs stayed quietly still.

The heartbroken silver dog let out a startled yip! It whined and whimpered beside its master, gasping. Its body shook involuntarily. It laid its head on Quenya, shedding tears, and made what appeared to be sobbing noises.

Even as a stranger, I could feel its grief over the loss of its master.

It was a terrible feeling.

I petted Silver on its back gently to soothe it.

"Quenya will forever be missed, especially by Silver," I whispered.

10

The blizzard finally died down a bit.

I searched through Quenya's possessions and found a map. It showed me how to get to Lorthic Castle and the Golden Wood.

"I will promise you to bring Anglachel back to the Guardian of the Golden Wood." I made a promise before I departed.

I glanced at the sword but then had an uneasy feeling.

Why did Quenya condemn this as an accursed blade that should be silenced? What is the history behind this blade?

Just when I picked up and unsheathed the sword, Silver leaped backward and snarled ferociously at the sword.

Then a miracle happened.

I saw a wisp spirit slowly rise from the body of Quenya.

"Guide the stranger... " the wisp said in a ghostly whisper. It encircled Silver as a shimmer of mist, diffused, before being absorbed by Anglachel.

The accused blade glowed bright red, before returning to normal color again.

What just happened? I felt puzzled.

I examined the sword.

It glimmered beautifully under the dim light of the lantern. It is a legendary weapon from hilt to blade. Along its sharp edges were inscribed with Elvish patterns. Whoever forged it must be a legendary blacksmith.

I buried Quenya behind the snow hut and followed the map down the hill to the village of Kukur.

My sabatons sank in the snow as I walked, leaving a trail of footprints behind.

Silver was following me.

I was not sure if the dog trusts me enough to be a companion yet. It kept a distance from me all the way.

Well, maybe it takes time to get over the loss of its master.

The road curved lower as we travelled past a frozen bog.

Beside me, I could see snow-covered shrubs and jutting rocks.

The sky quickly turned evening dark.

Two crows fluttered off their tree limb and soared away.

Soon, I arrived at a ledge.

I shielded my eyes with one hand and gazed up.

Apparently, Kukur is just up ahead.

The sun began to sink lower behind the snow-covered peak of a mountain. And the sky quickly darkened.

We better make it to the village before it gets any darker.

Who knows what awaits us in the dark after sunset.

An icy wind blew the swirling withered leaves at us as we continued to walk downhill. Gnarled trees creaked and groaned. Their scraggly trees shivered. Their bare limbs waved at as, as if trying to warn us away.

I smelt death within this place.

A while later, we saw an orange light flicker from a wooden light post up ahead.

The village should be close.

We followed the ragged dirt path, trying to stay away from the ledge. Broken urns and planks were scattered on the ground, unattended. Wagons and wooden carts were flipped upside down.

I wonder what happened.

Silver sniffed the ground restlessly and began to lead me.

"Silver, wait up," I yelled as it plunged wildly and suddenly went off by itself.

I followed the dog from behind, trying to keep up with its pace.

Then the familiar wooden gate of Kukur appeared. Two torches were lit on both sides.

A couple of men-at-arms were patrolling. Archers were standing inside the watchtower. They were young, about my age.

"Halt!" one of them shouted at me when he saw me approaching with Silver.

Suddenly, everyone's attention was on me.

"Stranger, where are you from? You don't seem to be

one of them," the men-at-arms asked.

"I am an adventurer. I am looking for my friends and the way to the Lorthic Castle," I replied. "Did you see three adventurers?"

The men-at-arms shook their head.

"I saw a dark wanderer headed towards the direction where you come from a few days ago." A voice spoke from behind with an Indian accent.

It was a child. He wore a purple vest and white trousers. It almost reminded me of the character in Aladdin.

The men-at-arms kneeled down as their master spoke.

"I am Prince Lorthic," the child introduced himself. "Please don't tell me you are another one of those treasure hunter and tomb raiders."

"No…no. I am not a treasure hunter. I am looking for my brother and my friends. We come to aid you, Prince Lorthic." I made myself clear.

"Very well. But, I am afraid I couldn't see the face of the dark wanderer as he was hooded with black robes. Could he be one of your friends?" Prince Lorthic asked.

Black hoods? I wondered who could that be.

"I…I have no idea." I shook my head.

A long, mournful howl from nowhere interrupted our conversation.

"Come, Stranger, follow me inside. It is not safe in the woods at night." Prince Lorthic gestured at us to follow him.

11

I followed Prince Lorthic into the village.

Silver was darting left and right to study the surroundings.

The roads were rugged and dirty.

I can hardly believe how Prince Lorthic ended up in this place.

Medieval houses made of stones and straw were encircling the town hall.

In the middle of the town hall was a bell tower overlooking the entire village.

We passed a wagon overloaded with mountains of bodies. The smell of the dead invaded my nostrils. Soldiers were busy directing peasants to move bodies to a burn pit.

Grieves and moans filled the place with dread.

"Your Highness, what had happened to Kukur?" I asked.

"A few weeks ago, a horde of demons, known as Hellspawn, invaded Lorthic Kukur. Villagers were massacred. Many of them fled. This all began when my father ordered his lieutenant, Antarial, and his elite army to venture a hidden secret in the Monastery of Kukur – we called it our cathedral," Prince Lorthic replied.

"Why would your father do that?" I questioned.

"There were rumors saying massive amount of treasures were buried beneath our cathedral since the ancient times. My father believes in it," Prince Lorthic said.

"What happened to Antarial and the rest of the elite army?" I pursued.

"Antarial and the rest of the elite army never returned. Some rumors said they escaped with the treasures. Others said Antarial ran into trouble and called for the King Lorthic's help, but my father didn't answer. Ever since Antarial's disappearance, strange moans were heard from within the cathedral. Sad moans. Inhuman moans. Someone even spotted hidden creatures lurking in the shadow of the cathedral," Prince Lorthic explained.

"Your Highness, how did you end up here?" I was curious.

"Lorthic Castle was under siege, swarmed by Hellspawns. I…I was supposed to wait for the reinforcement from the Elves to arrive in Kukur. Now, our supply is running short. I wonder what is taking them so long to come," Prince Lorthic uttered a long sigh.

I recalled how Quenya died defending the invasion of the village of Kukur…

"Your Highness, I am afraid the Elves reinforcement won't come…" I muttered.

"Pardon me." Prince Lorthic frowned. "Have the guardian of the Golden Wood changed her mind?"

"No. No. No. It is nothing like that. Quenya, the lieutenant of the Golden Wood, and his army was ambushed by Antarial," I said.

Prince Lorthic grieved for a moment, then his expression changed.

"Antarial was once a great champion of Lorthic. She helped my father in countless battles and built this kingdom. She is like a sister to me. She saved my life before…I will never believe these rumors," Prince Lorthic rejected.

I felt stupid. I did not know Antarial had such great bond with Prince Lorthic.

Maybe I just know too little as an outsider.

Villagers kneeled to greet the prince as we continued along the trail.

I could smell the fear among them.

Some of them were whispering about whether to stay in Kukur. Others were preparing to flee.

We came across the mayor of Kukur, who appeared to be putting up a wooden barricade to block the exit.

"Mayor of Kukur, what on Earth are you doing?" Prince Lorthic asked.

"M-m-my Prince, I …" the mayor stammered.

Then we saw the mayor's belongings and his sash of gold beside him.

You are right. He is abandoning his town.

"Do you know you will block others if we ever need to evacuate?" Prince Lorthic was angered.

"I ….I was thinking this might slow down the Hell-spawns from invading…" the mayor tried to find an excuse.

"Anyone can leave, but you and I will be the last ones staying in Kukur. It is our duty," Prince Lorthic commanded. "Dismount these barricades now!"

The mayor had no choice but to obey.

I must admit, even though Prince Lorthic is only a child, he has the spirit of a wise king. I think he will make a great king one day.

I continued to follow the Prince to the exit of Kukur.

We were back in the woods again.

Two bodyguards lit their torch and followed behind us.

"What can I do to fight the Hellspawns?" I offered my help.

"I admire your valor. But, I am afraid there is little you can do." Prince Lorthic sighed.

"Why don't you travel back to Lorthic Castle and call for reinforcement?" I suggested.

Prince Lorthic didn't reply.

But, it didn't take long for me to find out.

My mouth dropped open when I saw the great bridge connecting Kukur to Lorthic Castle demolished. The destruction looked like it was caused by a natural disaster.

"This is why we are on our own," Prince Lorthic said as he pointed to the fallen bridge.

12

The big bell tolled in a peal.

The rooster crowed just before the crack of dawn.

I didn't get much sleep last night.

Prince Lorthic said the destruction of the bridge was caused by a falling star, which also reduced the monastery in Kukri into ashes.

I began to recall what happened that night.

I kept thinking about Mike and my friends.

I wonder where they are now.

Will they become some type of characters in the game, too?

Silver looked depressed all night. I guess it takes time to get over the loss of its master.

When the morning finally came, I went to the town hall with Silver.

Prince Lorthic was giving a speech on the stage. He said he would send most of his troops to protect those who want to leave. They will be resettled as refugees in a kingdom west of Kukur. The prince urged the refugees to deliver a warning to other kingdoms to prepare for the invasion of the Hellspawns.

When Prince Lorthic was asked about his own plan, he said he would defend Kukur until the very last moment and delay the Hellspawns from catching up with the refugees.

Many villagers shed tears when they departed.

I had what I believe to be my first and last breakfast in Kukur. It was called mameliga – an egg-plant stuffed with forcemeat. It was a sensational dish.

Of course, I will never forget to feed Silver. It hopped up and down around me. Its tongue hung out of its open mouth. Its saliva dripped like a waterfall.

Cluck. Cluck.

A few chickens next to me pecked each other to fight for food.

I tossed a handful of forcemeat on the ground. The chicken bumped each out of the way and dipped their scrawny head for food.

"Stranger, have we meet before?" A girl's voice appeared from behind me. It sounded like a beautiful melody.

When I turned around, I saw a girl with a red Corsair's overshirt and white skirt. She had curly brown hair and silk-like ivory skin. Her liquid brown eyes locked on me, studying me with her serious look.

I recognized her. She was the girl sneaking in the Monastery of Kukri that night.

So, she survived the blast, too?

"Maybe we have. Maybe we haven't. What is your name? Why don't you join the rest of the villagers and escape this rotten place?" I asked.

"My name is Gabriella. I grew up in this town. I will die fighting for it," Gabriella replied with a British accent.

I almost burst out in laughter when I heard she said she wanted to defend Kukri. Gabriella's outfit reminded me more of a scholar than a warrior.

"What is the matter? What is so funny about it?" Gabriella felt annoyed.

"Just to let you know this is no place for peasants. You should join the others and leave," I mocked.

"Peasant? Is that what you think I am, stranger?" Gabriella choked. "Now, tell me. Who exactly are you? Why are you here?"

"I am nobody. I am just an adventurer, who comes to aid the Lorthic Castle. But, I lost all three of my friends during the journey," I explained, hiding the fact about what happened in the monastery that night.

"I don't believe you." Gabriella studied me. "So, are you going to defend Kukri, or are you are just another spy of demons?"

I realized Gabriella had the face of an angel but the heart of a barbarian.

"Why are you accusing me as a spy?" I frowned.

"You might be able to disguise it in front of Prince Lorthic because he is a child, but you can never escape my eyes. I will keep an eye on you." Gabriella glared at my sheathed sword.

"Do whatever you want." I rolled my eyes and walked away with Silver.

I wandered around the village and came across a blacksmith. He had large busy, mustache all over his round-cheeked face. His arms were big, with powerful muscles.

It seemed like he is the only blacksmith who stayed behind.

He was busy forging welding metals in high temperature and hammering them together. There were dozens of perfect swords hanging on the walls in his Blacksmith forge. A sword was glowing reddish orange inside the charcoal forge.

When I passed, the blacksmith looked at me with his green eyes. His mouth twisted in an unnatural grin.

"Greeting, stranger, you got a special weapon there." The blacksmith gestured him to come over.

"My name is Wayland. I have forged weapons for the Lorthic all my life." The blacksmith introduced himself.

"Greeting Wayland, what is so special about my weapon?" I was curious.

Just as I was about to unsheathe Anglachel, a high-pitched shriek from behind me almost made my heart stop pounding.

13

When I turned around, I saw Gabriella stared at me angrily.

"Hey darling, what are you up to?" Wayland shouted.

"This fool has no idea what he will unleash." Gabriella came over.

I dropped my mouth open.

What did I do?

"The sword you are holding is no ordinary sword. It is called Anglachel – a sword that contains great power, yet, great evil." Gabriella fared her eyes at me.

"What else do you know about this sword?" I asked.

"I am surprised the owner of Anglachel knows nothing about its history," Gabriella mocked.

"I am not the owner! I am on a mission to return this sword back to the Golden Wood." I lost my temper.

Wayland stood there, speechless.

"A couple of centuries ago, there was a rumor in this humble, small town of Kukri. An ancient evil was slayed by a group of heroes, and its soul was trapped within a magic moonstone beneath the Monastery of Kukri. The heroes warned the village to guard the monastery and ordered no one ever to go inside. When the heroes explored the lair of the ancient evil, they discovered treasures and gold. One of the items is Anglachel," Gabriella explained

"But that doesn't explain why Anglachel is an evil sword," I protested.

"The story doesn't ends here. Anglachel had consumed the souls of men and demons for centuries. Even the Hellspawns are terrified of it. It is said that those who wield Anglachel, wield absolute power. Many wars were fought to control that power, and many lives were lost…" Gabriella continued.

I gazed at the blade.

My heart was pounding with every word Gabriella spoke.

Is that true?

Is Anglachel really like what she said?

"No one knows the specifics of Anglachel's origin. Anglachel fed on the blood and soul of the slain ones. If left unfed…" Gabriella stopped halfway.

"What will happen then?" Wayland and I asked at the same time.

14

Gabriella didn't reply and shied away.

"What a strange girl," I whispered.

"Gabriella is tough and mean on the outside, but warm and caring inside." Wayland coughed. "She read too many stories."

Gabriella gave Wayland a sharp gaze.

"I better get back to work." Wayland walked clumsily away.

Suddenly, Anglachel began to vibrate.

Gabriella and I looked at it in silence as the sword began to glow.

"Something is coming," Gabriella whispered.

The next moment, we heard snarls and growls fill the mountain.

Groups of ravens rattled as they flocked away from the copse of trees.

Silver raced towards the entrance of the village and barked at the pathway where we came in.

Gabriella and I looked from behind.

Everything was so misty at the mouth of the groves.

Villagers outside the gate of Kukur were hovering in fright. They were discussing whether to abandon their refuge and get back inside the village.

"My mommy always tells me that there are no monsters, no real ones. But, there are," a little boy told his sister.

Prince Lorthic joined his generals in the guard tower above us. He ordered all his army to come forth to the entrance.

"They all have fear in their eyes," Gabriella whispered as she looked at the villagers and soldiers.

"I suggest you get back to the village. You look more like a scholar than a warrior," I told Gabriella.

"Really? I have lived longer than you may think," Gabriella replied.

Silver kept barking fiercely at the curtain of white up ahead.

Suddenly, a humanoid figure staggered and stumbled its way out of the misty woods.

Then another.

And another.

Some of them still had their Lorthic armor, while others were dressed in shredded and stained peasant clothes.

"Your Highness, it is Eric. He is one of us. He...he survived," a solider proposed.

The air was still.

Prince Lorthic watched indecisively as more figures appeared from behind the mist.

"Your Highness..." the solider urged Prince Lorthic to save them.

But, something isn't right.

Prince Lorthic watched them die protecting the village from the Hellspawns.

Why do they still live?

When Eric finally revealed himself from the mist, the children uttered a loud scream.

His-its-face was decaying. Flaps of dried skin hung from its sunken cheeks.

With a gasping moan, its peeling fingers grasped one of the defending soldiers and lunged for his throat.

15

Zip! Zip! Zip!

A first arrow from nowhere hit the creature in the throat, and it let out a dying scream. The second embedded it in the creature's ankle, causing it to collapse onto its knees.

The defending soldiers released from the creature's grasp did a quick slice with his sword.

The creature's head fell from its shoulder.

"They reanimated the dead as Hellspawns," Prince Lorthic cried in disgust. He drew his sword and ordered the bowmen above to reload and fire.

Arrows were showering the incoming Hellspawns like rain.

I joined the soldiers at the front line to fight.

But there were simply too many of them.

Gabriella took out a wand and waved it high up in the air. She muttered some strange words of magic. Her eyes glowed bright white. Everyone looked back at her as her wand was radiant with red yellow, and blue flames that danced from one hand to another.

"Formidable," Prince Lorthic stammered as he saw the magical energy begin to glow.

Everyone backed off immediately as Gabriella unleashed her deadly blow.

The magic extinguished the incoming enemy into ashes.

The villagers paused for a moment, and soldiers uttered a victorious cry.

Gabriella gasped. Sweat poured down her forehead.

Prince Lorthic came down from the watchtower to greet her.

"Yo-you are a sorceress," Prince Lorthic stammered.

"Magic," Wayland huffed under his breath from behind the crowd and giggled.

"Your Highness…" Gabriella kneeled down weakly to greet the prince.

Just as everyone thought the threats were over, the top of the icy mountain began to thump, sending shockwaves of mini-earthquakes that shook the ground.

THUD THUD THUD

"Wh-What was that?" one soldier asked.

"It felt like a glacier collapsed," another soldier speculated.

"But Kukur has no records of any glacier collapsing throughout history…" a peasant replied.

All of us gazed up and saw something was moving among the pine trees.

Whatever it might be, it must be something big.

The howling wind began to pelt us with hard, icy snow.

It was chilling cold.

Anglachel turned crimson red. The color glowed more intense by the second.

"Get everyone back inside the village," Prince Lorthic ordered when he sensed the shockwaves intensify.

Everyone was silent for a while, anxiously listening.

The thudding sound finally stopped.

Everything went silent like time had stopped.

I squinted into the misty entrance to the icy mountain.

My body numbed in the freezing white.

Snow swirled around us

My heart was pounding.

"Ooooh!" the crowd let out a startled cry when everyone saw a giant figure emerging from the curtain of white.

16

The colossal creature stood twenty feet tall. It had the torso of a beautiful women and hooves of horses. Four spider-like tentacles with talons extended from its back. Its long white hair stood on end.

"Antarial?" Prince Lorthic's mouth dropped open in horror. He couldn't believe his eyes. The once great champion, who vowed to protect Lorthic, had turned into a hideous monster.

The creature moved a few steps forward and loomed over us.

Its eyes were filled with rage.

"Your Highness, she is no longer the Antarial you used to know," Gabriella warned. She appeared weak. Her mana still hadn't recovered.

"Antarial, what happened to you? What happened that night beneath the cathedral?" Prince Lorthic shouted from a distance.

Antarial ignored the prince. It uprooted a palm tree with its claws and used it as a club.

"Look out!" I pulled Prince Lorthic away as the creature waved its club at him.

"Protect the prince!" the soldiers let out a war cry, and they began to charge.

Antarial waved its club again and sent a group of soldiers flying down the ledge of the mountain.

A group of bowmen from the watchtower attempted to shoot the creature from above, but was frozen from head to toe by Antarial's geyser of ice from its mouth.

Gabriella fired a few magic bolts with her wand, but Antarial dodged them easily with its superior dexterity.

Antarial's roar was like a thunderstorm. It huffed blizzard and frosty mist that shattered the approaching soldiers into fragments of ice!

"It is too strong for us." Gabriella dropped to her knees in despair.

"Pitiful," Antarial mocked us.

"Take the prince to safety. Fall back! Fall back! Down the mountain" a commander ordered.

"No. I am not leaving." Prince Lorthic loosened my grasp and went to confront the creature by himself.

"You are not Antarial! She would never do such evil thing!" Prince Lorthic cried bravely.

Everyone watched in horror as Antarial towered over the prince. It almost reminded me of David and Goliath in the Bible.

"Prince Lorthic, what can one little man do?" Antarial sniggered.

"You are not touching him." I walked in front of the prince.

"Oh really. And who is this nobody?" Antarial snickered.

"He is my friend. Why are you turning against us? Why are you massacring the people you vowed to protect?" Prince Lorthic demanded.

"King Lorthic is a ruthless and cruel warlord. That night, the king did not send us to treasure hunt like the rumor said. We were on a secret mission to steal a moonstone that was rumored hidden beneath the Monastery of Kukri. The king was desperate for that moonstone, because he believes it can give him power," Antarial explained.

"What kind of power?" Prince Lorthic asked.

"The power of immortality," Antarial replied.

"What happened in the monastery that night?" I asked.

"By the time my nine companions and I entered the deepest part of the monastery, we activated the abyss by accident and released Master Beelzebub from its seal. Knowing that we must save the city of Kukri, we fought the abyss. We did send one of us to seek the King's reinforcement. We continued to fight until we perished, but the reinforcement never came. One by one, I saw my elite companions being incinerated by the dark flame. I felt betrayed. When I was about to face my fate, Master Beelzebub sucked away every last part of my humanity," Antarial explained.

I felt sympathy for Antarial.

One man's craving for more power created such formidable rage.

"I am serving Master Beelzebub's Legion. I am rebirthed to bring destruction until every last man in Lorthic perishes. Even with the help of the Elves, you will never get past me and stop master Beelzebub's invasion.

The age of men is coming to an end. Now, prepare to die!" Antarial uttered a furious cry as one of its tentacles struck at the defenseless prince.

Without hesitation, I drew Anglachel and thrust it up high in the air.

17

Everything happened too fast.

Before I realized it, Antarial's tentacle split in two.

"Agh!" Antarial cried in pain.

Dark blood was dripping from the edge of Anglachel.

"We will meet again," the wretched creature shot me a sharp glance and escaped back into the snowy mountain behind it.

"Thank you for risking your life protecting me." Prince Lorthic came over.

"Your Highness, it is my duty," I replied.

I looked at the dark blood as it slowly disappeared from Anglachel.

"I wouldn't be happy too early," Gabriella came over and spoke.

"Anglachel has awakened and will spill the blood of your enemies. It must continue to feed on the souls of the slain. Each death will strength its cursed blade," Gabriella said.

"What if it doesn't feed?" I asked.

"Then it will devour the life energy of its wielder and

kill him. I regretted I didn't tell you earlier. I fear for your life." Gabriella felt remorse.

Does that mean my own weapon will kill me? This is complete nonsense.

"Even if this fairy tale is true, I will not regret saving the Prince," I replied.

"Very well. Perhaps you have the heart of a patriot. I may have misjudged you," Gabriella apologized. "Travelling past the icy mountain, and past the Keep of Antari-al, there is a legendary place called the Golden Wood – the homeland of the Wood Elves. We will seek help from the Guardian of the Golden Wood. I believe she is the only one who can help you to remove this curse now. I will lead you there."

"May I accompany you?" Prince Lorthic joined.

Gabriella and I looked at each other for a long moment.

"No. Your Highness, it is too dangerous," I kneeled and cupped his hand in mine. "But, I promise you we will make Kukri safe again."

"Very well, I shall give you my guards. Please, be safe," Prince Lorthic said as he ordered some soldiers to protect us.

Gabriella and I gathered enough provisions and thanked the prince.

"Can you promise me one thing," the prince said, just as we were about to head off.

"Yes, your Highness." I said.

"Ca...can you promise me not to kill Antarial. I hope you can release her from her misery." Prince Lorthic begged me with his watery eyes.

"You still want her live after she tried to kill you?" I frowned.

Prince Lorthic nodded and handed me a small vase.

"Th-this is divine of blessing," Gabriella exclaimed. "It is a magical flask filled with holy water. Rumor says that divine of blessing can cleanse a wretched soul."

"Thank you, young prince. I promise you," I said.

We said farewell and began to ascend the mountain.

18

Gabriella led me and five other guards up the snowy mountain.

Silver was following beside me.

Snow trickled down my face. The cold burned my skin.

Sometimes, I wondered if Silver felt cold at all.

We had already walked five miles out of the village. When I looked back down, I couldn't see anything but snow and sky.

We followed the enormous, deep footprints left by Antarial.

The deep snow crunched under our feet.

"Antarial Keep should be up ahead." Gabriella returned her head.

"I will whack her with my battle axe like a knife through hot butter," another soldier laughed.

"Really? But, where were you just then?"

"He was cowardly, hiding behind Prince Lorthic."

The soldiers laughed among themselves.

Gabriella shook her head and continued.

Silver paused for a while when we passed by the same snow hut where it lost its master.

We traveled a couple more miles. I squinted through the sheet of white falling snow and saw the steeple of the same ice tower I saw.

"That tower must be where Antarial hides." The soldiers pointed at the tall tower a couple of miles away.

"This tower used to be an outpost of Lorthic guarded by Antarial. Who would have imagined it becomes the monster's lair today?" A soldier sighed.

We continued to walk as the tower loomed over us. Its black windows glared into mine like evil black eyes.

"Hold," Gabriella shouted suddenly. She looked puzzled when she looked at the last footprint in front of her.

"What is it?" I hurried over and asked.

Gabriella tilted her head to look at the tower and crouched low to study the last footprint.

Silver was sniffing frantically beside where Gabriella stood.

Suddenly, I had a bad feeling. A very bad feeling.

I scanned the horizon of the jagged mountain but saw nothing but a curtain of white. The clouds had blanketed the sun.

The snow came down harder and faster. The howling wind pelted us with hard, icy snow.

All a sudden, I felt something manipulating the weather.

"Stay close. We could easily lose each other in the blizzard," Gabriella warned.

Suddenly, the ground gave way beneath our feet.

One of the soldiers lost his balance and fell into a crevasse in the snow that opened a deep pit.

"Help!" the soldier's voice trailed off as he fell deep into the freezing white.

"Hang onto each other," I screamed at the top of my lungs, but it was overwhelmed by the howling wind.

Gabriella tightened her grip on my armor to show she understood my message.

Powdery snow continued to swirl around us.

The weather made it impossible for us to proceed.

Before we decided to turn back, I heard a low rumbling sound.

"Di-did you hear that?" a soldier asked in a trembling voice.

Before we could find out what was happening, the whole ground began to shake. The rumbling soon became a roar as the snow wall began to crack and crumble.

The snow roared down from the icy tower like a monster.

It was an avalanche.

"*Oooooh* no!" I uttered a startled cry as I felt myself being sucked beneath the snow.

Snow piled over our heads.

Silver yelped and barked, trying to keep its head above the snow.

I couldn't see where the others are anymore.

When the next wave of snow tumbled down on us, all we could see was a high wall of white and gray.

***

When I recovered my consciousness, I discovered myself lying on a pile of snow.

A chunk of snow fell off the pit wall. It landed on the top of my head and made me shiver.

I looked up and saw the opening of a crevasse thirty feet above.

No sunlight reached the bottom.

I spun around but there were no signs of others.

I tried to grab onto the jutting rock and fumbled for a foothold. But, my hands slipped and slid back to the bottom.

How can I ever climb out of here? Will I freeze to death?

I felt moments of dread and despair.

Bluish icicles of different shapes were hanging from the ceiling.

I spun around and saw a dim glow of blue behind me.

A passageway? Where may this lead?

I followed the light.

The only sound I heard was the drip of the melting icicles.

Anglachel began to glow red again.

I arrived inside a chamber where there were dozens of human snow clones. Their bodies were frozen solid, like statues. Their eyes wide opened in fright.

This must be the work of Antarial…

One by one, I examined the human snow clones closely.

Why does Antarial have to keep these human snow clones deep below the icy mountain?

Then a familiar face caught the corner of my eyes.

"Mike?" I dropped my mouth open in disbelief when I

saw my brother.

I couldn't believe my eyes when I saw my brother turned into a snow-covered statue. His body was solid ice from head to toe.

My heart was pounding fast.

Cold sweat trickled down my forehead.

What has the creature done to my brother?

A high-pitch screamed of a lady from the far end of the chamber interrupted my thoughts.

The next thing that happened was an explosion of ice and freeze.

19

I tried to move, but my legs were frozen.

I watched in horror as Antarial sprayed a shard of ice and turned its victim into snow clones.

I squinted and stared some more.

It ...it was Gabriella

She was being frozen like the others.

I tried to move, but a chuck of ice froze my left leg.

Do something to save her. I urged myself.

"Hey! I am here, you wretched queen," I yelled to the demon.

"Hah! There you are." Antarial snarled at me and flexed its neck. "It is about time you showed up."

"I came to finish off my unfinished business. Get back here," I yelled.

"Is that so?" Antarial sniggered. "You rushed headlong to me without thinking about the consequence."

Antarial walked toward me and the ground thudded.

"Why did you turn everyone into snow clones," I asked.

"These snow clones will be my gifts for Master Beelzebub." Antarial laughed. "Soon, you will be one of them."

Antarial took shards of broken ice from the ceiling and fired at me.

I ducked as the projectile whizzed past my face.

Antarial angered as it missed.

It summoned an ice bolt and hurled at my chest.

Slice!

I wielded Anglachel in a flash of speed, and the ice bolt was split into two.

Look out!

Gabriella screamed in terror as Antarial leaped towards me with a wild scream. It swiped its giant paw at me for a lethal attack.

I tried to leapt back, but I couldn't move.

I watched in horror as the black figure of the demon loomed over me.

All of a sudden, I heard a hoarse voice.

It was the accursed blade … It was Anglachel.

Magic is not as...powerful as many think. Sometimes, a good sword arm can be as valuable as a hundred spells. I will teach you how to unleash its true power.

All a sudden, Anglachel took over the control of my body. It seemed to have a mind of its own. Precisely, my mind was no longer my own.

There was blood and fury in my eyes as I thrust Anglachel in the air.

The next second, I saw the demon shriek in pain and collapse onto the ground.

Blood scattered everywhere onto the white ice.

Antarial tried to summon its ice magic, but I involuntarily raised Anglachel and chopped it like a lumberjack gone mad.

Antarial staggered a few steps back.

Blood was dripping from its wound like a river of red.

"Ho-how is that possible?" Antarial cried weakly as its magic began to fade.

The ice that imprisoned my leg began to melt.

Chunks of snow dropped from the human snow clones. They thudded on the floor, melted and disappeared.

They're defrosting. I realized.

Just before I finished the demon, I heard Silver howl thirty feet from above.

Sun beamed down in the opening of the crevasse.

Then I saw Prince Lorthic and his guards hoist themselves down the snow pit.

"Please don't kill Antarial. Save her," Prince Lorthic cried in a distance as he hurried towards me.

Finish it…finish it now… feed me with its demonic blood…

"Huh?" I tried to regain control of my body, but I couldn't.

Prince Lorthic and everyone watched in horror as I start to pour the divine of blessing onto the ground!

"Why did you do that?" Prince Lorthic looked at me in disbelief.

Antarial lay defenselessly on the ground, gasping hard, dying.

Kill it... kill Antarial ...

The voice echoed in my head, and I began to feel pressure and pain.

I tried to battle it with my subconscious.

But, the pain throbbed violently in my head such that I felt like my skull was going to split.

Against its kind, there could only be blood for blood.

20

With one final struggle, I let go of Anglachel and picked up the flask of divine of blessing.

I quickly splattered the remaining holy water onto the fallen demon before Anglachel had a chance to mind control me again.

"Argh!," Antarial cried in pain as the holy water burned its skin.

It staggered around aimlessly as if it caught fire.

Everyone watched in silence as a sparkling field of ice and snow surrounded Antarial.

The demonic features of Antarial began to shrink. Its spider-like tentacles withered and collapsed onto the ground. Its claws and hooves shape-shifted back to arms and legs.

"Thank you, warrior," Prince Lorthic thanked me as Antarial transformed back to her human form, once again.

He ordered his guards to shelter Antarial with furs and clothes.

"Thank you for releasing me." Antarial squinted at me.

She whispered weakly and then fainted.

Gabriella walked towards me from the far end of the chamber.

"You did well," Gabriella forced a smile. "Thank you for saving us."

"Yo!" A familiar voice cried from behind me.

It was Mike.

"Huh? Is that you, Tom? How come you are here?" Mike staggered all the way to reach me. It seemed like the cold had drained all his energy.

"Yes. It is a long story," I replied as Mike collapsed onto me, exhausted.

"Your brother is cute." Gabriella smiled.

"He is cute when he is not arguing. I wonder how he ended up being trapped in this hideous cave," I replied.

Prince Lorthic commanded those outside the snow pit to lower ropes.

Everyone in the pit leaned against the pit wall.

Pull. The crowd shouted.

Slowly, one by one, we were hoisted up to the top of the crevasse.

I looked at the accursed blade on the ground.

Clearly, it wasn't me who defeated Antarial. I know that something controlled me.

Perhaps, I should bury it here and let it be forgotten.

"You must take it with you. And you will bring it back to the Golden Wood. I know it is a huge burden. But, we cannot allow Anglachel to fall into the hands of enemies," Gabriella warned.

"Perhaps, you are right." I uttered a long sigh and reluctantly picked up the blade.

Everyone celebrated as we got back to the village.

Wayland waved us a welcome gesture as we went back to the village again.

Prince Lorthic replaced the old mayor with a new one.

The horror that haunted Kukri is no more.

The villagers worked together and began to rebuild the village.

I had a great supper with the crowd that night.

Everyone celebrated the victory.

Everyone praised me as the Defender of Kukri.

That night, Prince Lorthic walked me to the demolished bridge that was supposed to connect Kukur to Lorthic Castle.

"I saw your incredible strength. I hope you can help my father and save my people," Prince Lorthic asked.

I hesitated and looked at my sword.

"Your Highness, I …I am afraid it is not a duty I can handle," I finally spoke.

"Is it because of the sword?" Prince Lorthic glanced at Anglachel.

"I must return it to the Guardian of the Golden Wood," I replied. "Only the elves can have the magic to silence this accursed blade."

"Very well. If this is the case, I wish you could be my messenger. The North of the Golden Wood is the Capital of Zhorm. There is an ancient conqueror, a great ruler, who had the strength of a thousand men. His name is Ciema. In the past, this champion helped to defend Lorthic as the first line of defense. He vowed to protect his own people in the Capital of Zhorm above anything. But, over time, his people doubted him because he was different. He did not receive the respect and love he deserves. I wish you can help me to awaken this patriot to fight for Lorthic once again," Prince Lorthic said.

"Your Highness, leave it to me. I will find Ciema and join force with him to resurrect Lorthic," I promised.

PART 3

21

Gabriella, , Mike, Silver, and I ventured past Antarial Keep and headed East.

I looked at Mike's deserter outfit.

He almost reminded me of a thief.

He can't blame me calling him names because he loves to sneak around all the time. He had a bandit's knife in his pocket and an iron round shield and a short bow at his back.

We walked a couple of miles and finally reached the peak of the snow-covered mountain.

I squinted into the far distance but couldn't tell where the mountain ended and the clouds began.

Everything seemed like we stepped into some kind of fairy tale.

"Don't worry, we will reach the Golden Wood if we continue to head East," Gabriella suggested.

"Silver is from the Golden Wood, so it knows the way," I said as I saw Silver sniffing at the ground and led us the way.

We hiked one summit and another.

Soon, we saw green!

Yes. We saw everlasting green just below the cluster of clouds.

"We are finally out of the snow!" we cried happily.

Mountain goats lifted their heads to look at the unexpected guests as we walk past.

We must have disturbed them from eating the grass.

High up in the sky, falcons were scanning for food. Their whistling cries proclaimed domination over the sky.

Silver raced off to the mountain crest without glancing back. Its tail was waving back and forth.

"Wait up, Silver!" I screamed behind it.

"Maybe you should get a collar," Mike joked.

We hurried behind Silver.

By the time we reached the top of the mountain, we saw an endless forest from below. It was showered by the golden ray of the sun.

It was magnificent!

"This is the legendary Golden Wood. We are officially in the territory of the Elves," Gabriella said.

"Have you been here before?" Mike asked.

"Of course. Everyone who practices magic must travel through the Golden Wood," Gabriella replied.

"Magic…you know magic?" Mike raised his eyebrows.

"Yes. Gabriella knows magic. She knows very powerful magic. I saw it with my own eyes," I added.

"Can you teach me?" Mike pleaded.

"Hmph….." Gabriella studied Mike for a while and declined. "You'd better not. Sorcery is not for everyone.

And should not be forced. You have your own strength and talents. Sorcery need not be one of them. Don't let it bother you," Gabriella denied.

"Fair enough." Mike sighed.

We descended all the way down the steep, grassy slope of the mountain.

By the time we reached the bottom, we arrived at the opening of a cypress tree tunnel.

An enormous black bird peered at us from a low branch of a cypress tree. It cawed at us repeatedly, as if to warn us to go away.

Silver seemed to be cautious rather than excited.

"My intuition is telling me there is something different about the Golden Wood," Gabriella speculated.

"Why is that?" Mike asked.

"I have no idea." Gabriella studied the environment. "Even though this is the territory of the Elves, dangers are everywhere in the wood. So, keep your eyes open."

Under the deep shade of the trees, a squirrel hopped from trees to trees, creating the sound of crackling twigs.

We continued our way through the forest.

I knew I was not here for sightseeing, but I couldn't take my eyes away from the eerie-looking typography of the trees.

I have never seen trees so tall in my life.

I wondered how old they are?

Can they be hundreds or even thousands of years old?

We huddled together as we walk deeper into the wood.

Occasionally, we could hear the shrill of the insects

and crow of the birds.

We pushed ourselves through tall, leafy ferns and arrived at the bank of a creek.

I could hear the soft trickle of the running water from the creek bed.

"Water?" Mike whispered. "I heard the water from the Elf are magical."

Just as Mike was about to feel the water, Silver uttered a low growl.

The dog's body stood tense, revealing two sharp rows of jagged teeth and barked at the creek.

"Huh?" I was surprised when I saw Anglachel glowed red.

"I think Silver senses danger," Gabriella said softly.

22

Suddenly, dozens of giant leeches emerged from the surface of the creek. Their long fat bodies were squishy, inching towards us.

Look out!

I screamed in horror as they leaped at Mike, who stood just a few meters apart.

Mike dodged quickly.

The leeches slammed onto the ground in front of Mike. They wriggled and squirmed.

"Not too shabby," Mike said gleefully as he stabbed his bandit's knife into the closest leech.

Purple, poisonous mucus splattered all over Mike.

"My eyes!" Mike shrieked in pain as he backed off.

Before I could help, a squishy sound from behind me made me turn my head.

I tilted my head and saw dozens of leeches raining from the trees.

"It is a trap," Gabriella shouted as she urged us to leave.

Silver barked at us and led the way.

I wrapped Mike's arm over my shoulder and followed Silver.

We staggered and tumbled all the way as we tried to escape the deadly trap.

Tall grasses brushed against our waists.

The scraggly limbs of the trees waved at us, as if trying to warn us to leave.

To be honest, I never thought the Golden Wood was filled with danger. After all, this should be the territory of the Elves.

We stopped after travelling miles into the wood.

I wished I had a compass; when I looked back, everything appeared to be the same.

"Tom, I…I can't see," Mike said in a low, frightened voice.

"This is no good. He is poisoned by the mucus," Gabriella came over and looked at him. "We have to find the Elves as soon as possible."

"But, we do not even know where we are. Are there any ways we can slow down the poison for my brother?" I asked nervously.

Suddenly, the sound of a fart interrupted our conversation.

"Mike, is that you? Are you releasing poisonous gas?" I speculated.

"No way," Mike protested.

Then I looked at Gabriella, and she shrugged.

We squeezed our nose as the smell of the fart invaded our nostrils.

Silver looked at me with its innocent eyes.

Another fart from behind us made us turn around.

Surprisingly, we saw no one.

So, who is farting?

I kneeled down and brushed the shrubs away.

Shafts of sunlight revealed a red giant mushroom as tall as my waist. The mushroom had a pair of bizarre eyes and nothing else.

It appeared to be as astonished as we were when it saw us.

"Invaders of the Golden Wood, please do not kill me," the giant mushroom pleaded.

"Whose voice is that?" Mike asked.

"I bet you wouldn't believe it. It is a talking mush-room" I replied.

"Don't worry. We are not invaders. We won't hurt you," Gabriella replied. "Can you help me? Where can I find the Guardian of the Golden Wood?"

"Uh-oh. The Guardian...um... I know where she is. But I don't think you want to go there," the giant mush-room stammered.

"Why?" I asked hastily. "We have a person to save and something crucial to return to the Guardian."

"If I were you, I will leave the Golden Wood and nev-er return again," the giant mushroom warned.

"What happened to the Golden Wood? Isn't it pro-tected by the Elves?" Gabriella asked.

"The Golden Wood used to be protected by the Elves. Not anymore. Everything changed ever since a dark wanderer passed by and headed North through the wood. Unknown perils lurk in the murky depth of the wood. Ogres and trolls roam freely in the woods. Even the Great Grey Wolf is on the loose. The Elves are in deep trouble right now. I don't think they have time for guests," the giant mushroom explained.

Did it say a dark wanderer? I remembered Prince Lorthic once said that all the tragedies began to happen when a traveller hooded with black ropes travelled past the village of Kukri.

I wondered who he is.

"I don't care. Nothing is more important than this." Gabriella pointed to Anglachel.

"And this." I pointed to Mike.

"Anglachel? I thought it is sealed by the Elves. Oh please…get this sword away from me. The Elves are in the North. Follow the white wisps, and they will show you the way," the giant mushroom said, and it tried to turn away from us.

"Thanks a lot, mushroom. By the way, do you know how to cure my brother's poison?" I asked.

"The purple moss clump can save your brother's life. The Elves will have them. Good luck. Hopefully, we will never meet again," the mushroom replied and ended our conversation with a fart.

How disgusting!

23

We continued to venture North.

The air felt sticky against my face.

Trees with big brown trunks tilted over one another to form some weird typography.

Scratchy board leaves brushed against our body as we made our way through the forest.

We followed a narrow path with a cluster of ferns and trees.

Suddenly, Anglachel glowed bright red again.

"What the?" I was surprised when Anglachel unsheathed itself and flew to the sky.

I dropped Mike onto the ground.

Look out!

We watched in horror as Anglachel turned around in mid-air and struck at my heart with full speed.

I dodged.

Anglachel dashed past me as I grasped it by the handle immediately.

I wrestled with the accursed blade as it tried to break loose.

Gabriella and Silver tried to come over and help, but an invisible force pushed them away.

The accursed blade drained my life energy, and I collapsed onto the ground, still holding it firmly.

A moment later, Anglachel was silenced again.

"My worst nightmare has come true. The curse of Anglachel has begun." Gabriella sighed.

I gasped for breath.

My body felt so weak. It felt like all my stamina was drained.

Silver looked at me sadly.

"Anglachel must be fed or else it will continue to devour the every last bit of life energy from its wielder," Gabriella warned.

"So, are you telling me to continue to kill anybody just to save my life?" I questioned in a weak voice.

"I am sorry. But, this is your curse. We must find the Guardian to lift the curse from you before it is too late." Gabriella came and pulled me up on my knees.

"What curse? Can someone tell me what is going on?" Mike worried.

"Your brother is sick. We will heal him," Gabriella replied.

After a while, my breathing slowed to normal again.

"I think we better get going," I insisted.

We followed Silver as the ragged path curved deeper into the wood.

Birds chattered noisily on the branches above us.

Some small creatures were scampering noisily in the shrubs.

A light breeze made the leaves scrape and creak.

"Are you all right?" I asked Mike.

"Yes. I am barely alive," Mike replied weakly.

It was getting dark. We trudged miles and miles North but couldn't see a single elf. It made me wonder where the Golden Wood could be.

"Look! Wisps," Gabriella exclaimed as she saw thousands of tiny white wisps flutter above the shrubs, casting light, glistening like little diamond.

Silver raced to the wisps as if it saw its old friends. It chased them around in a circle, wagging its tail.

"Magnificent." I joined Gabriella as I saw the sparkling wisps play gleefully with one another.

It looked like the scene of a fairy tale.

"The wisps are known as spirit of the Elves. Perhaps, I can communicate with them to find out the location of the Golden Wood, just like what the mushroom said," Gabriella suggested.

I nodded.

Gabriella waved her wand in the air as colorful particles danced with her gesture. Her eyes closed. Quickly, the wisps floated to encircle her. No one spoke a single word.

I wondered if this is what people call telepathy.

I watched Gabriella silently as her expression changed.

Drops of tears traced down her wobbling cheek.

Is Gabriella crying?

What is going on?

Just as I began to walk towards the sobbing sorceress, the wisps scattered as if I was an enemy.

Falcons peered down at me from a cypress tree. They

cawed, as if telling the forest to beware of my presence.

Something isn't right.

"Gabriella, can you please tell me what is going on?" I demanded.

ZIP!

An arrow sank into a boulder beside me, just missing me by an inch.

I tried to evade but was stopped by a booming voice.

"Stop moving. I promise you the next arrow will pierce right through your heart," the voice warned.

"Show yourself," I yelled.

Then I felt a big shadow loom darkly from behind me.

Before I could move a muscle, I felt a pair of strong arms grab me from behind.

24

It was a living tree!

I watched in horror as two sturdy branches grabbed me by the arms. Other smaller branches reached out to slap and whip me.

Another branch wrapped around my right leg.

It formed a knot and hung me upside down.

"Let me go! Let me gooooo!" I begged the branches that trashed me wildly.

The more I tried to break loose, the tighter the grasp became.

I watched helplessly as the branch pulled me into the center.

The humanoid creature stood at least fourteen foot high. It has the head of an oak tree. Its skin resembled tree barks. It sturdy trunk revealed the face of an old man. Its glittering eyes locked on me with anger.

"What kind of tree are you!" I shouted.

"Tree? I am no tree. I am an Ent – the protector of the Golden Wood." The Ent angered.

"Well…well…well, look who we have got here - a sorceress, a blind thief, and a human with demonic scent. How intriguing." An elf uncloaked himself from behind a tree.

"Who are you?" I tried to struggle, but the Ent was too strong.

"I am Amr, the captain of the Elves. Do you have any final words, intruders?" Amr declared.

More Elves revealed themselves behind the trees.

"Wait! There must be a misunderstanding. We are not intruders. We come and seek the help of the Elves," I defended.

"Then how can you explain why you possess the demonic blade? Humans are deceptive and filled with greed. You must have sided with the ogres and trolls, and ambushed my brother, Quenya, while we foolishly sent aid to your wretched King in dire need," Amr mocked.

"This is not true," Gabriella shook her head.

"It is not for you to decide. Bring them back to the Guardian," Amr ordered.

Just before we marched off, Silver revealed itself from a shrub.

"Silver!" Amr was astonished when he saw the dog.

It looked like his long lost friend.

The dog raced towards the elf. Its tail wagged. Its eyes sobbed.

Amr petted and soothed the dog, as they communicated telepathically.

After a long while, Amr turned to me again.

"I … I may have misjudged the three of you. Silver told me everything about you. Please accept my apology," Amr apologized.

Ent slowly kneeled down and released me.

I brushed the twigs and leaves from my armor.

Amr commanded a few wisps to encircle Gabriella.

"What are they doing?" I asked suspiciously.

"They are restoring the mana they drained from your friends. Wisps are spirit of the Elves. Once we die, our spirit turns into wisps. Wisps can dispel magical buff and drain mana. Like the falcons, they are also our eyes and ears in the woods," Amr explained.

Then I recalled Quenya's spirit being sucked to the accursed blade when he took the form as a wisp.

"So, you have been monitoring us?" I asked.

"Yes. We have been keeping an eye on the three of you ever since you stepped foot in the Golden Wood. But, it is not the wisp that drew our attention to you. It is your demonic presence – it is Anglachel," Amr said.

A group of birds fluttered off the tree limbs and cawed with fright.

"I think the Great Grey Wolf may be near; we better leave," Amr said as we regrouped and headed towards the heart of the Golden Wood.

25

The Ent scooped up Mike, Gabriella, and me and sat on its shoulder.

Silver went on foot with the rest of the Elves.

I really need to thank Silver for this.

Without its help, our adventure could have ended here.

We gazed at the sky on top of the Ent. The orange sun was sinking behind the horizon of the woods.

The sky was a mixture of purple and crimson red.

It was like a silhouette art.

Everything was so beautiful.

"I wish I could see," Mike sighed as Gabriella described the scene to him.

I am a bit surprised to see they get along pretty well.

After a while, we arrived at a majestic village surrounding a gulf. White elven buildings and architecture were adjacent to each other. Behind the village were huge mountains with tall waterfalls supplying water to the village. When a shaft of orange sunlight beamed down the village, everything looked lush and green.

Everything is a heaven of incredible natural beauty.

According to Amr, elves are capable to live up to thousands of years. They are inherently magical and have a high level of civilization.

We departed the Ent at the entrance of the village.

Then we followed Amr across an arch bridge.

Amr motioned us to gaze at the gulf on our left. It was a great harbor view with elven ships. The elves were busy offloading containers after a cargo ship boarded.

"The elf merchants used to do a lot of trades with the Capital of Zhorm. But the trades were severely interrupted ever since the Golden Wood was invaded by the ogres and trolls," Amr explained.

"How come an invasion interrupted the trades?" Mike asked.

"We no longer recommended our people to go into the woods alone anymore. We can see through the eyes of the ravens that the enemies are lurking in the woods. When we have gathered nothing, we have nothing to trade," Amr answered.

I cupped my hand around my eyes to shield from the light to see further.

"I saw there are only a few human ships in the harbor," I said.

"I know. I have realized it too. The trade is slowing down fast. I wonder if the Capital of Zhorm faces the same fate we have," Amr guessed.

We continued our way up.

Soon, we arrived in front of a majestic garden.

Colorful wisps were dancing around restlessly as they saw us.

They sparkled and left behind traces of fading particles of different color.

It was magnificent.

But, Gabriella didn't seem to appreciate it. She huddled behind us the whole time.

I know what she is worrying about. She fears the wisps will drain her precious mana again.

"This is the territory of the High Elves, where the Guardian of the Golden Wood lives," Amr said. "This is a rare opportunity. Not many people can meet the Guardian like this."

"Aren't you coming with us?" I said.

"I am afraid I have to go back and patrol the borders, my friend. " Amr smiled.

When we stepped in the garden, we felt an unknown energy sweep over us.

We felt warm and vibrant.

Standing in front of me was a tall lady of extraordinary beauty and dressed in purest white. She had silk-like skin. Her long river of hair shone the golden color of the sun. Beautiful, sparkling wisps were dancing around her. As she approached me, the aura of her lordliness radiated.

"Your Royal Highness," we said and knelt respectfully.

"I know who you are. I am the Guardian of the Golden Wood. Few have spoken my name. Lorthic has fallen … the covenant between men and elves is broken … the fire fades…"

I think I have heard this before.

But what does the Guardian mean by Lorthic has fallen? Are the elves and men no longer allies? Which fire is fading?

I followed the lady as she guided me to the inner part of the garden.

Up ahead, I saw a spectacular silvery mirror dish.

It was filled with water.

A parrot with vibrant color landed beside the mirror. It was studying me with suspicious eyes.

"Come." The lady motioned me over to look into the mirror. "Let the mirror guide your way."

As I stepped forward, the clashing sound of my armor scared the parrot away.

The lady took her flask and slowly poured water onto the mirror.

I lowered my head and glimpsed.

Everything looked so clear, so real. My reflection clearly revealed that I had aged.

The sound of the pouring water continued.

Slowly, my reflection distorted.

The ripples soon blended the vision of the mirror into something...

Something different ...

My eyes opened wide.

I could no longer see myself but terror approaching.

I heard screams.

I saw destruction.

I saw the kingdom of Lorthic was under siege. And villages, one by one, were burning in flames.

I saw the innocents fleeing helplessly and the lords surrendering their thrones.

The magnificent statue of Lorthic crumbled into ashes.

Oh wait. It was Irina, a daughter in the royal family of Lorthic! She was held captive and guarded by scythe-wielding wraiths.

My heart was pounding fast as I saw my once-peaceful homeland in flames.

Next, I saw an unfathomably powerful demon, whose body was a combination of fire and ice crystals. This frightening destroyer infiltrated the High Wall of Lorthic Castle unchallenged.

The inferno from the demon made me force myself to step back from the mirror.

"Your Majesty, what…what happened?" I stammered.

"Lorthic needs you," the Guardian said.

"But…I cannot do this," I spoke weakly. "I hope you can help my brother to see again. I hope you can help me to lift my curse - my curse from Anglachel."

The Guardian sprinkled traces of sparkling particles onto Mike's face, and Mike slowly opened his eyes.

"I can see again! I can see again! Thank you my majesty. Thank you," Mike cried happily after the Guardian restored his vision.

"My Majesty, I am returning Anglachel to the Guardian of the Golden Wood. This is my promise to Quenya…" I kneeled down and said.

The Guardian studied me for a long while and finally replied.

"I may not be able to lift this curse."

26

I was devastated.

I was hoping the Guardian could help.

"My majesty, but why?" I questioned.

"You must hurry to Lorthic Castle. There is a powerful sorcerer locked inside the dungeon, guarded by demons. Free him. He is the key to Anglachel's curse," the Guardian said as she revealed the appearance of the sorcerer.

Although the image was blurry, somehow, I felt the sorcerer looked familiar.

Where have I seen him before?

"My Majesty, can you please tell us what is the fastest way to travel to Lorthic Castle from here?" Gabriella asked.

"You will take one of the merchant boats and head to the Capital of Zhorm. Follow west and you will find Lorthic. You must hurry. May the God be with you," the Guardian said.

We thanked the Guardian for her advice and headed outside the garden.

By the time we were back to the elven village, we heard a bell toll.

Elves in plated armor marched down to the entrance of the gulf. Their expressions were serious.

"What is going on?" Mike wondered as the tensions were building every second.

Anglachel began to glowed red again.

"Something is attacking the Elves," I speculated.

We followed the Elves to the entrance.

Even from a distance, we saw the forest incinerating.

I watched in anger as the Ent that carried us to the elven village was captured and being burnt alive in front of the Elves. It moaned and crumbled into ashes.

Next to it was an army of barbarians and muscular raiders with green skin.

"What are these?" I asked the nearest Elf warrior.

"These are the Hordes – a green army of orcs, goblin, ogres, and trolls. They are scourges of all civilization. They have no direction or purpose other than simple violence. They love only wars," the Elf warrior explained.

The trolls continue to throw liquid fire and cause destruction.

The once magnificent homeland of the Elves turned into inferno advents of flames.

Amr slipped an arrow from his quiver, and the arrow embedded in the neck of the troll.

He blew his horn. And the archers rain down countless arrows to the Hordes.

"Forward!" a green ogre with a twisted face and pointed teeth grunted.

Ogres and trolls growled and snarled as they

swarmed the defending Elves.

"This will be the end of the elves," a goblin uttered a horrible laugh.

Dozens of orcs wolf riders jumped across the Elves' defense and bypassed them.

Mike spun around and spotted a troll sneaking behind a little elf girl. Its yellow eyes glittered. Slowly, it opened its mouth and jagged teeth to feed.

Zip! Zip! Zip!

"Eat this instead." Mike swiftly fired an arrow and opened a hole in the troll's forehead.

Gabriella's hands were bright with energy, sending one missile after the next.

Clang! Clang! Clang!

The Hordes pushed the Elves to the upper level of the village as they continued to charge.

More orcs swamped from the woods to invade the elven village.

"This is not going well. We cannot hold. There are too many of them." The Elves trembled.

I wanted to join the frontline to fight alongside the Elves, but a voice stopped me.

Kill them. Kill them all. Massacre with the unyielding sword of Anglachel. Slay any living things. For that is our curse.

27

"Do something!" Gabriella urged as her mana was depleting.

Just when Amr ordered the rest of the Elves to retreat to the garden, dozens of wolves leaped in front of him and blocked the entrance.

Without warning, the wolves swung their big paws at Amr.

Amr ducked just in time as the nail nicked his face.

Before the wolves made another leap to the fallen elf, I unsheathed Anglachel and pointed it at the wolf riders.

"Well, well. Look who we have here," a wolf rider spoke and the rest of the troops turned their attention to me.

"A wretched knight," another wolf rider joined. "You can't be serious. But, I'd like to see you try."

I gritted my teeth as a dozen giant, frenzy wolf heads turned to me with a mouthful of razor sharp teeth.

Are you afraid of a few pitiful wolves? Swing me!

I swung Anglachel as the wolves leaped towards me. I swirled the blade to wolf riders. A minute later, not one man stood except me.

It surprised me that the more I killed, the more energetic I got.

The enemies roared at me angrily from below as I broke their formation.

Eight armored ogres the size of apes swung their spiked mace as they sent the Elves sky high. They grunted while their lips curled over their ivory teeth.

With little effort, the ogres broke the Elves' front line of defense and pressured us to move up.

A group of elf archers focused fire at the ogres, but their arrows deflected from their thick armor. They stood in the front line as the rest of the Hordes marched from behind them.

"If we keep on falling back, we will be pushed back to the Garden soon," an elf said.

Amr recovered from the wolf's attack. He gazed at the entrance of the Garden, but the Guardian still had not revealed herself.

"Trust the Guardian," Amr insisted. "Have faith in her."

Mike swallowed hard when he saw the river of Hordes just crossed the bridge into the elven village.

"We are outnumbered," Mike whispered.

Just when everyone felt dread and despair, we heard a beautiful melody played by an elven flute. The music was clear but sorrowful. It reminded me of a lonely elf playing a flute under a tree at night.

My heart felt peaceful all of a sudden.

Surprisingly, the melody seemed to influence the Hordes as well. They stopped their attack as if they had entered a hypnosis state.

"Leave the Golden Wood and never return again," the Guardian demanded.

"Leave? Master Beelzebub walked the Earth once again. The forest is withering away. The magic of the elves is diminishing. Our victory is at hand. Soon, we will conquer the Capital of Zhorm – the last stronghold of human race," an ogre leader shouted.

The Hordes grunted in triumph.

"Master Beelzebub knows in advance you will interfere with our invasion, so he prepared a present especially for you," a goblin scoffed and motioned us to the entrance of the elven village.

THUD THUD THUD

The whole elven village seemed to quiver and shake.

My heart was pounding.

What is it? What is the goblin taking about?

"Is it an earthquake?" Mike's voice trembled.

We watched in horror was the trees began to shake.

Twigs and branches snapped loudly in the air.

"An earthquake does not shake like this. Something is moving towards the elven village. Something huge," Gabriella whispered.

We heard grumbles and growls somewhere in the distance.

I turned my head and saw the elves swallow hard, sweating all over.

I wondered what could make even the almighty elves tremble.

THUD THUD THUD

I vaguely saw a gigantic figure stomp through the trees. It was so tall that it almost reached the height of an oak tree.

Gabriella, Mike, and I huddled together. Trembling.

I wondered where Silver is right now.

The figure slowly entered the far side of the clearing.

Everyone watched in horror as a gigantic, long snout revealed itself at the misty entrance of the elven village. The monstrous nostrils flared in and out and began to sniff.

28

Panic swept over the elven village as the creature revealed itself.

"It...it is Fenris - The Great Grey Wolf," the Guardian seemed surprised.

The beast opened its jaw. Saliva was dripping like a waterfall. Rows of jagged teeth rose up from its purple gum. The ground trembled each time its fury paws hit the ground.

"Oh no! How did it find its way to the elven village?" Amr choked out.

"Please go back into the wood," one of the elves prayed, sweating.

Fenris's tail wagged back and forth. It banged against an elven hut, and demolished it into rumbles.

My body tensed as the beast crept in our direction.

"The Great Grey Wolf almost destroyed the elves before. It will destroy the elves again. Kill them. Kill them all!" the goblin commanded.

"Hey weaklings, who do you think should be in command?" an ogre said as it knocked the poor goblin off the ground.

Dozens of goblins snarled at the ogre. They banded together to thrust their hunting spear at their giant cousin.

All of a sudden, the Hordes sparked a civil war among themselves.

"What?" the elves watched in joy as the trolls and the ogres fought against one another.

"The Horde is a very uncoordinated race. Their tribes have been known to fight each other. They are their own worst enemy," the Guardian said.

Soon, the goblins decided to withdraw from the battlefield. They fled to the arch bridge but saw Fenris blocked their way.

"Get out of our way, you stupid big wolf!" a goblin shouted at the gigantic beast.

Without warning, Fenris lowered its head to feed.

The goblin screamed in terror as Fenris chased after them like a cat chasing mice.

"Fenris is betraying us!" the last goblin shrieked as the Great Grey Wolf threw it in midair before ending in its stomach.

The Hordes panicked when they saw the goblins were annihilated.

I squinted at the clearing and saw something else emerge from the far side of the clearing.

The figure revealed itself behind Fenris.

"Silver?" I dropped my mouth open when I saw my friend standing behind the almighty beast.

"It is your fault! We could have defeated the Elves ourselves. Whose idea it is to summon such a deceptive beast. Now, we are cornered!" the ogre roared at the orcs and trolls. "Charge at the Guardian!"

The Guardian muttered some strange words of magic. Her eyes glowed bright white. The sky began to crackle.

Bolts of lightning descended from the sky, just when the Hordes were about to charge.

The eight armored ogres were electrified in the blink of an eye.

"For the Guardian of the Golden Wood! Avenge the Ents!" Amr unsheathed his sword and commanded his elven troops to drive the enemies far away.

29

" Y ou saved our lives once again!" I raced over to Silver.

The dog panted when it saw me. It hung out its tongue and wagged its tail.

"It saved the Elves," the Guardian descended and joined us at the arch bridge.

I kneeled down to soothe the dog.

Then I tilted my head to look at the gigantic wolf looming over me.

It made me wonder what is the relationship between Silver and Fenris.

Why did it save us?

"Long time ago, an ancient elf was on a mission to slay a demon Lord in the abyss. The ancient elf took his two loyal battle companions, Fenris and Silver, and ventured into the abyss. They succeeded in slaying the demon, but the abyss was closing faster than expected. The ancient elf knew that not all three of them could escape. So, he attempted to use his remaining power to erect a cleansing barrier to buy time for his battle companions to escape," the Guardian explained.

"What happened next?" I pursued.

The Guardian looked at Fenris with her sorrowful eyes.

"But, both Silver and Fenris have chosen loyalty. They went back for their master. At the last moment, when the abyss portal was closing, Fenris bravely kicked Silver out of the portal, while it continued to battle the Abyss…" the Guardian continued.

I felt sorry for misunderstanding the Great Grey Wolf.

I would never have expected Silver had such a tragic past. The loss of its masters must have scarred its heart.

"Is that how Fenris became so big?" I asked.

"Indeed. Over time, Fenris defeated the abyss. But the dark energy transformed it into a terrifying beast. It hated the elves for not coming to rescue its master. It attacked everything in the Golden Wood, until it met Silver again…" the Guardian explained.

"Perhaps, it is time for them to have a reunion," I replied.

"Indeed," the Guardian whispered.

Later that night, Amr and the rest of the elves prepared the rebuild of the elven village. They invited us for supper, mainly sugar-cane berries and fruit. Unlike many people believe, not all elves are vegetarians. Some had roasted meat on an open fire. Some had mushrooms, rabbits, frogs, and even tree barks for supplements, which turned my stomach.

The next day, the Guardian had arranged for us to board a merchant ship, returning to the Capital of

Zhorm.

Gabriella, Mike, and I waved farewell to Silver and our elven friends. We departed the magnificent place.

We enjoyed staring out to the sea.

The water was calm, shimmering like gold under the morning sunlight.

I wondered what danger could lie ahead of us.

PART 4

30

We sailed in the deep blue ocean for days.

Our provisions began to run low.

We talked to the steersman to find out how far the Capital of Zhorm is; apparently, he said we should have reached there yesterday. It was the direction of the wind that has been delaying us.

The waves bounced our ship.

I gazed at the fogged ocean and couldn't see where the sky actually began.

To be honest, it can be scarier looking at the infinite ocean, wondering if you will ever arrive at your destination. The sea can sometimes generate fear and uncertainty.

Mike vomited into the ocean as the wave continued to drift us back and forth. I never knew my brother had seasickness. Oh well. Perhaps, it is because we have never been in the middle of the ocean before.

"This is no good," the steersman gestured to the heavy, low clouds that blanketed the sky.

Our eyes followed his gesture.

Sure, it is not okay; it looked like a thunderstorm is approaching.

The howling wind blew our sail canvases violently.

Soon, the sky was darkening.

Streaks of lightning flashed in a zig-zag pattern. The next minute, we heard thunder roar the sky.

"Wow. Can our ship survive the weather?" Mike wondered.

"Do you have other options than to stay?" the steersman replied.

Heavy rain pattered. Waves crashed into us.

"Hold on! A big one is coming," the steersman screamed as a giant wave tossed us in the air.

We were totally soaked.

Half of the ship was filled with water.

We hurried to grab buckets and scoop out the water. But the merciless waves soon filled the ship with water as soon as we emptied it.

"Don't let go! Don't give up. We can make it!" Gabriella shrieked over the hostile weather.

We huddled with each other, enduring the adversity as best as we could.

I squinted my eyes and tried to look ahead, but the visibility was too low.

My fingers felt numb, but I couldn't let go of the rail. If I let go, I would be gone for sure. I had no choice but to endure.

Another wave tossed our ship high.

The next moment, we heard our steersman's scream trail off as he was thrashed right into the ocean!

"Nooooooo!" I tried to reach out for him, but I was

too late.

Now, our ship was floating freely in the storm.

"I can't believe it. We survived the most horrifying beast, but we can't survive the madness of the weather," Mike complained.

Heavy rained continued to hammer us without mercy.

Suddenly, we vaguely saw blurry light behind the curtain of the storm.

The three of us squinted in the flickering light as it approached us.

Puzzled.

What is it? What can it be?

31

It…it was a giant ship!

No. It was a pirate ship!

The pirate ship loomed over us, as it skulked through the mist by the light of the silvery moon.

"A merchant ship!" One of the pirates with an eye patch and a cutlass pointed at us from above.

"That means there will be gold and treasures on their boat!" Another pirate grinned, showing his stained, uneven pirate teeth.

"Lift them up. Take everything they have got." A third pirate in a red velvet jacket and pirate hat commanded. His left arm was missing and was replaced by a silver pirate hook. He looked like the captain of the ship.

Several pirates hoisted themselves down ropes and took everything, including us, back to the pirate ship.

"Well…well…well, look who we have got here - a sorceress, a thief, and a knight," the captain mocked and the rest of them joined the laughter.

I was so exhausted.

Gabriella and Mike were already unconscious by the

time they were on board.

The flickering light on the pirate ship made me dizzy.

Everything looked blurry around me.

I knew I will collapse any minute.

I gazed at our merchant ship as it slowly sank into the depth of the ocean.

"Captain, we found nothing valuable on the merchant ship. Should we throw these people back to the ocean to feed the sharks?" a pirate voice muttered.

The captain slowly walked towards the three of us and grinned.

"No. Tie them up. Search their bodies. Maybe we can find something valuable." The captain grinned as he punched me in the face.

The next thing I saw was black.

32

I don't recall how long I was unconscious.

By the time I reopened my eyes, everything looked different.

I was no longer on a pirate ship.

The truth is that I don't even know where I was.

It looked like some kind of cave...

When I tried to move, I realized I was handcuffed and tied to a wooden chair. I looked down and discovered my suit of armor was gone.

Everything...all my possessions were gone!

Anglachel was stolen!

This was not good.

I could never imagine what would happen if the accursed blade fell into the wrong hands.

My eyes darted left and right to search for Gabriella and Mike, but it seemed like they were locked away...

Suddenly, the melody of a whistle and laughter caught my attention. Then I saw a flickering light approaching from the entrance of the cave.

Slowly, a few staggering figures came into the distance.

Pirates.

"Oh dear, another wretched contender. Welcome to my camp, knight of Lorthic," the captain said, pointing his silver pirate hook at me.

"Where am I?" I asked.

"You are in the cave of despair. It is where we keep our prisoners and salves," the pirate spoke.

"Who are you?" I clenched my teeth.

"I am the almighty Crusade, captain of the pirates," the captain introduced himself. "And you must be sent by King Lorthic to root us out. I must admit I am quite surprised to see a knight from the South in a merchant ship."

"No. I am not sent by King Lorthic. I am an adventurer," I responded.

"Oh really? An adventurer in a suit of armor." Crusade laughed and his pirate followed.

"What is so funny? Where are my friends? Where is my sword?" I questioned repeatedly.

"Silent!" Crusade shouted, annoyed.

"I am serving Master Beelzebub's Legion. Your friends and the other wretched contenders cannot sail across the Sea of Zhorm under my watch. I will not let you pass. In just a few more days, Master Beelzebub will unleash Hellspawns to Lorthic. When that happens, Crusade will retake the Capital of Zhorm!" Crusade said as he unsheathed Anglachel and pointed it at me.

I watched Anglachel as it began to glow red again.

"Huh? What is happening?" The other pirates' eyes wide opened in fright.

"What kind of sword is this? How come it glows in red?" Crusade was puzzled.

"It is a demonic blade that will devour the life energy of its wielder and kill him. I am an adventurer travelling to Lorthic for a cure. I regretted I didn't tell you earlier. Now, I fear for your life," I mocked.

"You are lying!" Crusade's hand trembled and let go of the sword.

THUD THUD THUD

Suddenly, the ground shook. Debris and dust collapsed from the ceiling of the cave.

A few pirates staggered and fell to the ground.

"Wh-What was that?" the pirates stammered. They drew their curved sword and froze in their position.

THUD THUD THUD

The sound became louder and nearer...

The whole cave seemed to quiver and shake.

What could that be? My heart began to pound as I watched Anglachel glow brighter and brighter.

"Hey, the two of you. Check out the entrance of the cave," Crusade ordered his pirates.

But the pirates looked back at him with a worried face.

"Why are you still standing here? Are you a tree? Get moving," Crusade demanded.

We watched the two pirates as they slowly disappeared in the abyss.

My eyes peered in the darkness. My heart was racing.

THUD THUD THUD

The ground shook again.

Before we could react, the next thing I heard from the

abyss was a bloody scream.

33

"Let's get out of here!" the pirate screamed, and they all scrambled to the exit.

"Come back here, you fools." Crusade stumbled onto the ground.

"You have lost control of them," I sneered.

"I am going to kill you before you say another word," Crusade angered.

Just as he was about to lift his silver pirate hook and smash it into my head, a magical purple ribbon tied him up and threw him into the cave.

Crusade was knocked out instantly.

Then I saw Gabriella and Mike.

"What was taking you guys so long?" I smiled.

"Brother, do you know what my skill is?" Mike asked.

"What is it?" I shrugged.

"My skill is lock picking. That's how we got out so quickly from the cell," Mike replied and untied me with his bandit's knife.

"Yes. A thief is not completely useless after all," Gabriella teased.

Shivers crawled up our spines when we heard a thunderous inhuman roar from outside the cave. The next thing we heard were the dying screams of the pirates.

"Wh-what is going on outside?" Mike stammered.

More dust and debris collapsed from the ceiling.

"I don't know. Whatever it is outside drove the pirates mad," I whispered.

"Whatever it is outside, we better hurry. It looked like the cave could collapse any second," Gabriella warned.

I looked at Anglachel and hesitated for a moment.

"I am afraid you will have to take it with you," Gabriella said.

"Yes. I don't have many options, do I?" I said as I retrieved all my possessions.

We followed the trace of the footprints and arrived at the mouth of the cave.

"He...help me," a pirate squeaked. Frightened. Slowly, he surrendered his weapons and pointed his trembling finger up.

"What is he doing? What is he pointing at?" Mike narrowed his eyes.

THUD THUD THUD

Without warning, something huge trampled on him. The next minute, the pirate was squashed flat!

The three of us hurried outside and arrived at a mountain ledge.

We watched in horror when we saw a gigantic humanoid in armor looming over us.

With a roar, the giant projected a spherical boulder and knocked three pirates down the ledge. Their screams trailed off as they fell down the abyss below the mountain.

"Wh-what is that thing." My mouth dropped open in fear.

The hulking giant's eyes glowed red, scanning for any living things. Its body and armor were covered with several burning scars and cuts. The giant machete in his right hand was like a hunk of raw iron.

"Look out!" Gabriella screamed as the giant turned around and swung its weapon.

The next minute, the tall oak trees above us were hacked and cleaved.

The giant turned to our direction. Its red eyes scanned left and right.

The three of us huddled with one another behind a boulder.

Every step the giant took made the ground tremble.

My heart was pounding so hard that it felt like it would burst out of my chest.

The giant continued to encircle our position.

Can it smell us?

It continued to wield its giant machete recklessly.

In just a short while, the part of the forest looked like as if it had a haircut.

"This is no good. It is just a matter of time before it can spot us." Mike worried.

Just when Gabriella attempted to take her wand to cast magic, a melody from a flute drew the giant's attention away.

The melody was so sad and sorrowful…

Who was that?

The giant turned away from us. It spun around and

was attracted to the source.

I tried to peer at the giant's face from below when it began to turn.

But I couldn't see its face. I saw the helmet on its head, which looked like a deformed crown.

THUD THUD THUD

Step by step, the giant made the ground tremble as it walked away.

The three of us poked our head up and watched the giant disappear behind the curtain of mist, up the mountain.

34

The three of us uttered a long sigh of relief.

The sky was darkening. We followed a ragged dirt path and made our way down the mountain.

Soon, we arrived in front of a gorgeous stone citadel shaped like the keel of a ship. The citadel towered like a bastion of white stone, with five levels, each was set as a wall. A large subtle and well-fortified ring wall encircled the citadel. Somehow, it made me wonder if this amazing architecture is the work of men.

We made our way to the tall front gate.

"Halt!" a gatekeeper shouted at us from the guard tower and made us stop. Soldiers spread out along the wall.

Dozens of archers were ready to cut down any unwanted intruders.

"It looks like someone is picking a fight," Mike whispered.

"We come from the village of Kukri. We were supposed to head towards Lorthic through the Capital of Zhorm, but lost our way in the sea storm," I said as the three of us lifted our hands up and surrendered our weapons.

"Well, strangers. This is the Capital of Zhorm," a familiar face appeared next to the gatekeeper.

"Isaac!" I cried happily when I saw my friend. He was a crusader.

"Huh? Tom?" Isaac's eyes opened wide when he saw me.

I never expected to meet Isaac.

Not like this.

Isaac commanded the archers to lower their bows. Then he descended the gate to meet us.

"The oracle told me the savior of Zhorm will come from the south. But, I didn't expect it…it is you. Please follow me." Isaac motioned us into the citadel.

We followed Isaac into the citadel. It surprised me to see the interior of the citadel was chaotic. Most of the buildings in the lower levels were reduced to rubble and debris. I could see despair in the villagers' eyes when they met my glance.

I introduced Gabriella to Isaac and told him she was the girl in the Monastery of Kukri. But, he seemed to have forgotten about what happened, as well as his real identity. He believes that he is a crusader serving the Capital of Zhorm …

We continued up the next few levels.

Wounded soldiers and knights were lying against the white stones, moaning in pain.

Then I recalled Prince Lorthic's words. It made me wonder what is happening to the Capital of Zhorm…

35

After a while, we reached the top of the citadel. Large government buildings, siege workshops, and barracks filled the open space. There was a fallen giant statue next to a half-finished pyramid-like structure. Hundreds of villagers were busy working on the construction.

We followed a stone path to the center of the level. There was a large outdoor fountain made of granite and marble. In the middle of the fountain were beautiful sculptures of angels.

A while later, we arrived at a large balcony that oversaw the Capital of Zhorm.

The view was magnificent.

The citadel was a castle surrounded by mountains and rifts. The South was a shimmering ocean that led to the Golden Wood. I could vaguely see a fading fire in a raised hill in the West.

"That is Lorthic Castle," Isaac pointed to where I glanced. "It was once a noble kingdom we vowed to defend. Now, hordes of demons roam the land freely. King Lorthic is pushed into despair…the fire fades…"

"Why is the army of the Capital of Zhorm not defending Lorthic?" I questioned.

"The army of Zhorm never had a chance to reach Lorthic." Isaac motioned me to the wounded soldiers.

"Prince Lorthic once told me there is a conqueror, called Ciema, a greater ruler with the strength of a thousand men. Why doesn't the Capital of Zhorm summon him to fight for Lorthic once again?" I frowned.

Isaac looked at the fallen giant statue and uttered a long sigh.

"What is it?" Gabriella and Mike asked together.

"Ironically, Ciema is the reason our army can never reach Lorthic." Isaac pointed to the mountain where we came from.

"Huh? What do you mean?" I asked.

"Ciema was an almighty conqueror, a ruler of the Capital of Zhorm. He had helped Lorthic in countless victorious battles. King Lorthic used him as his first line of defense until…." Isaac replied.

"What happened?" I pursued.

"Until those people Ciema vowed to protect doubted him, until the mantle of the Lord interested him none. Until the falling stars drove him into madness."

A deep voice came from behind us.

We turned around and saw an old man with a walking stick. He wore an eyepiece. His hairstyle reminded me of the famous scientist - Albert Einstein.

Isaac bowed to him with respect as the old man joined us.

"My name is Oscar. I am the oracle of Zhorm. I have been expecting the three of you to come," Oscar spoke.

147

"Old man, your hair looks…interesting. I wonder how old are you." Mike raised his eyebrows.

Isaac pretended to cough. He was signaling Mike to remain silent.

"Well, thief. Have a guess," Oscar teased.

"I might look like a thief. But I am a warrior in disguise. I think you are at least eighty," Mike guessed.

"I have to say you have a terrible guess, but I like your answer. I can foresee you playing a very important role to assist your brother when you reach Lorthic Castle." Oscar laughed.

"What is so funny?" Gabriella gave the old man an uneasy look.

"Oh, a sorcerer, why don't you have a guess too?" Oscar requested.

"I have no interest in such a childish game," Gabriella refused.

"You were an orphan, abandoned by your parents in the Golden Wood, and raised by the elves. Unlike your companions, your agenda to Lorthic Castle is very different," Oscar said.

"I am not sure what you are talking about," Gabriella denied.

"Time will tell," Oscar replied as he walked towards me.

"Do you want me to guess your age?" I sounded stupid.

"Killing is not the only way to rescue Lorthic kingdom. Sometimes, compassion can be your greatest ally," Oscar said as he gazed at Anglachel.

"What do you mean?" I asked.

Oscar didn't reply. He smiled and walked away.

"What a weird old man," Mike spoke.

"Oscar might be strange. But I suggest you take his advice. His words are filled with wisdom," Isaac suggested.

"How old is he anyway?" I asked irresistibly.

"Oscar is two hundred years ago. He lived in ages where empires rise and fall. To him, it is only history repeating," Isaac replied as he saw the oracle disappear among the crowd.

36

That night, I had a terrible dream.

I dreamed of the demonized version of myself massacring everyone in the Capital of Zhorm. I saw Anglachel glow bright red as it had completely taken control of my body and thoughts.

Then I woke up in the middle of the night, sweating all over.

My heart was pounding.

I still remembered how Anglachel unsheathed itself and drained my life energy in the Golden Wood.

I must head towards Lorthic Castle to seek the powerful sorcerer Guardian talked about as soon as possible. I must have this curse lifted before I do any harm to the innocents.

I decided to leave.

I walked outside the cabin. I gave Gabriella and Mike one last gaze before shutting the door. Apparently, they were sleeping soundly.

I descended the citadel level by level in the dark.

The silent night was interrupted by the sound of my

sabatons.

When I finally reached the bottom, I saw Oscar sitting next to the gate, his legs crossed, smoking a cigar.

"Have you finally understood compassion can be your greatest ally?" Oscar exhaled a question mark smoke pattern in the air.

I ignored the oracle and walked past him.

"That's fine if you decide to ignore my wisdom. We will have another sad soul lost in the mountain," Oscar murmured.

"Excuse me?" I asked impatiently. "I am just doing a favor for these people living here by leaving. This accursed blade is my own burden. It is consuming my soul. I must journey to the Lorthic Castle myself."

"You sound just like Ciema. He risked everything for his people in the frontlines. But, in a war, he lost someone important to him. He blamed himself for his inability to protect the people he loved. Then people began to doubt him. Ciema did not receive the respect and love he deserves. One day, a fallen star from the sky struck the Capital of Zhorm, destroying the city and incinerating the inhabitants. Ciema failed to protect his people, once again. So, he decided to hide in the mountain, distanced himself from the people he used to love." Oscar sighed.

"But Isaac said he attacked the army that was supposed to save Lorthic," I denied.

"Indeed. I am a dear friend of Ciema. Over the years, I observed the changes inside him. He once gave me a gift that can slay giants of his strength. He told me that, if he ever lost his mind and harmed his people, I have the obligation to slay him. But, I just couldn't do it…"

Oscar said as he handed me a broken blade.

"Why do you give me a broken blade?" I asked.

"No. This is no ordinary blade. This blade can bring giants to their knees. But I hope you never need to use it. Like I said, compassion can be your greatest ally," Oscar advised.

"Is there any chance I can avoid Ciema on my way to Lorthic Castle?" I asked.

"I am afraid it might not be possible," Oscar denied. "Ciema the giant can smell you from a distance."

I looked at Oscar for a long moment.

Suddenly, I had a plan.

37

"Come with me." I kneeled in front of the oracle.

Oscar's eyes wide opened.

"Ciema needs you," I continued. "I cannot do this without you."

"But, I can't face him…I don't want to carry out my pact with him," Oscar said reluctantly.

"Compassion," I placed my hand on my chest and then handed the broken blade back to him.

Oscar studied my eyes and finally agreed.

"To be in your presence is a great honour." Oscar's grin turned into a big smile. Wrinkles spread all over his face.

***

I followed Oscar as he led the way up the mountain.

I must admit that traveling with a two-hundred-year-old oracle on foot did slow me down quite a bit.

We travelled one summit after another.

Finally, we arrived in front of the opening of a massive temple supported by tall pillars. A long stone stairway made of decayed rocks towered above us.

Anglachel started to glow red as soon as we arrived at the entrance.

"Lorthic Castle should be behind this temple connected by a bridge. There is no other way around it without going through this temple," Oscar said.

"Fair enough," I said as I drew the sword and headed up the stairs.

By the time we reached the top, we saw a dark hallway with a very high ceiling.

The smell of decay invaded our nostrils.

Yuck!

"What is that smell inside the temple?" I asked.

Oscar didn't reply. He lit a torch and illuminated the interior of the hallway.

"This is no longer a temple. This is a catacomb," Oscar whispered. His expression saddened.

My eyes darted left and right as I followed the light.

It horrified me to see everything was covered by seared corpse, moulded deep into the walls and pillars.

"This is madness. What have you become, my friend," Oscar uttered a long deep sigh of despair.

We followed the giant footsteps.

Then we made a few more turns into long, twisted hallways to reach a chamber.

"Welcome to my thorn room. I am Ciema. The greatest conqueror."

A deep voice roared in the darkness.

"Ciema, is that you?" Oscar waved his torch, and we both saw a giant sat comfortably on his throne.

"You may have saved him once in the mountain. But,

I don't think you should save him again, old friend," Ciema roared.

Did Oscar save me?

I recalled the melody of the flute that distracted the giant for our escape.

"Ciema, why are you doing this? Where is the patriot who fought for Lorthic?" I shouted.

"My people will never appreciate what I have sacrificed for them. I won countless battles for Lorthic for justice. But, no matter what I do for them, I am different. I am still a giant!" Ciema cried in rage.

Its roar echoed so loud in the hallway that we were forced to shield our ears.

"No! Your people love and respect you!" I denied.

The hulking giant stood up from its thorn. It eyes glowed blood red.

THUD THUD THUD

Step-by-Step, it walked towards us, revealing its giant machete behind his back.

"No, my old friend, it doesn't have to end like this." Oscar shook his head.

"Oscar, get out of my way. No human can leave my thorn room alive." Ciema's red eyes locked on me with rage.

Its body and armor was covered with several burning scars and cuts.

Without warning, it swung its giant machete and smashed into a pillar in front of me.

I ducked and rolled to the side just in time before a large chunk of rocks collapsed onto me.

Before I regained my balance, the giant swung its

machete again.

I parried with Anglachel just in time, but the momentum sent me back straight to the wall of the thorn room.

Pain shot through my back.

I heard a loud crack and realized the back of my knight armor was damaged.

Beside me were piles of corpses, which were the soldiers supposed to assist King Lorthic.

"You are too weak," Ciema mocked.

THUD THUD THUD

The giant made the ground tremble as it made its way to me again.

Oscar raised his walking stick high in the air. He muttered some strange words of magic, and ribbons of purple energy wrapped around the giant's body.

Oscar is a sorcerer! I realized.

However, the purple ribbons did not resist the giant at all as it continued with its march.

It grabbed me with one hand and lifted me high in the air.

I was too weak to resist.

I watched in despair, as my body was lifted higher and higher above ground.

"Time to die," Ciema cried as it began to squeeze.

38

"Ciema, have you forgotten our pact?" Oscar screamed at the top of his lungs.

The giant turned around and saw a glowing blue aura lingering to the broken blade.

"Ciema, my friend, it is enough. Do not make me do this," Oscar threatened the giant.

"What do you know about my pain? What do you know about my suffering?" Ciema turned to Oscar and tightened its grasp.

"We…we understand you," I said weakly.

"What do you understand about me?" Ciema asked.

"Your people have mistaken you. You are not different. You are the champion of Lorthic. You deserve love and respect. Come back to us. Fight for Lorthic, once again. This is the message from Prince Lorthic!" I cried.

"Prince Lorthic?" Ciema released its grasp, and I landed hard on the ground.

"Are you okay?" Oscar came forward to help me get back on my feet.

"What is wrong with Ciema? Why did he release me

when I mentioned Prince Lorthic?" I asked Oscar.

"It is because Ciema saved Prince Lorthic numerous times. They have a strong bond," Oscar replied.

Finish Ciema…put him out of his misery…

A voice from nowhere echoed in my head, followed by a crushing pain.

"No…it is happening again," I tried to resist, but the pain was so intense.

"What is it?" Oscar tried to help, but I pushed him away.

"Get away from me!" I yelled.

Slay Ciema…slay him now, you fool…

"*Anglachel*, it has been a long time." Ciema focused on me again. Its voice came out hoarse and dry.

It swiftly wielded its giant machete right at me.

Clang!

Anglachel commanded me to parry.

But the formidable strength of the giant made me stagger.

Ciema tried to grab me again, but I did a backflip to evade his grasp.

I shifted under the giant and stabbed the blade in its thigh.

The giant roared in pain and collapsed onto its knees.

I tried to battle *Anglachel* with my mind, but the evil was taking over me.

"It is said that those who wield Anglachel, wield absolute power," I mocked involuntarily.

"We will see about that. You are going to pay, worm." Ciema quickly got back up to its feet.

It uttered a battle cry and the whole thorn room trembled. Chunks of debris and rubble rained from the ceiling.

"Don't harm Ciema. Remember compassion," Oscar cried one last time as a random giant rock collapsed onto him right in front of my eyes!

Before I could help, Ciema whirled with its giant machete and collapsed the two pillars to block my rescue.

"How could you do that...you murdered your own friend!" I cried in disbelief.

Ciema paused for a short moment when it saw its friend devoured by the rubble.

Then he scrambled towards where Oscar was buried.

Without warning, *Anglachel* loosened from my grasp.

"What the –" I was astonished when I saw the accursed blade sizzle through the air like a living thing and attempt to impale right into the heart of Ciema.

"Back! I am commanding you to stop!" I used my subconscious to decelerate *Anglachel's* strike just in time for the giant to dodge.

Then the blade dropped onto the ground.

You fool...

I quickly grabbed Anglachel and sheathed it.

"You...you saved me," Ciema said. Its red eyes were no longer filled with rage. The burning scars and cuts in its body slowly extinguished.

"I did not save you. I just feel sympathy for your past," I replied.

Anglachel continued to vibrate as if it wanted to do more harm.

With one final struggle to break loose, the accursed blade drained my life energy again, and I collapsed onto the ground.

You failed me again and again. Remember that I am the host. You are only my vessel. I will give you one last chance before I devour your soul...

A dark voice appeared in my head, and Anglachel was silenced again.

"Are you okay?" Ciema patted me on the shoulder, accidentally knocking me on the ground.

"I guess I will feel better once I leave this place." I rolled my eyes.

"Help me!"

A weak voice from the pile of rubble drew our attention.

The oracle still lived.

Ciema and I hurried to move the rocks and debris away. We saw Oscar covered with dirt and dust. His eyepiece was cracked.

"I am glad the two of you are not fighting each other anymore." Oscar smiled.

"Compassion." I smiled back.

Then, a familiar voice interrupted our conversation.

It was Mike, Isaac, and Gabriella.

"Stay away from my brother!" Mike had his bow

pointed at the giant.

Ciema put down its giant machete to show he meant no harm.

My friends hurried to me.

They looked rather suspicious.

"How did you tame the giant?" Isaac asked.

"It is a long story." I forced a smile.

39

Ciema led us to the temple exit and then we began to say farewell.

Oscar and Isaac said they welcomed Ciema to rebuild and lead the Capital of Zhorm, once again. Oscar threw the broken blade Ciema gave him off the ledge. He told the giant he would never need it again.

Mike kept looking at me.

"Why are you staring at me like that?" I asked.

"Don't you realize you aged a lot overnight?" Mike replied. "You look like Dad's age now."

"This is impossible," I denied.

"It is true," Gabriella replied harshly.

"The origin of Anglachel's curse is an ancient parasite that feeds on blood of the slay. If left unfed, it will consume the life force, youth, and vitality of its wielder if he resists to kill," Ciema explained.

I tried to touch and get a feel of my look. I could feel the wrinkles and loosened skin.

"You must venture to Lorthic Castle quickly. Free the powerful sorcerer locked inside the dungeon. He will be able to cure your disease," Oscar advised.

Ciema shielded its eyes as it stared at the Lorthic Castle to the West.

"Beware, Beelzebub summoned a river of Hellspawns. They are prepared to launch the final attack at the Lorthic Castle. I fear you might not have much time," Ciema worried.

"Will you fight for Lorthic?" I asked the giant again.

Ciema went silent.

"No. I will answer King Lorthic's help no more." Ciema angered and turned away.

"All right, giants have strange attitudes." Mike raised his eyebrows.

"We will head back to the Capital of Zhorm and regroup. I hope Lorthic can stand until our reinforcement arrives," Isaac said as he said farewell once more.

***

It was a damp morning.

Gabriella, Mike, and I continued to head West.

I lifted my eyes to the sky. There were no puffy white clouds. No sun.

Everything looked grey and lifeless.

"Lorthic Castle should be just up ahead," Gabriella said.

An icy wind blew down the hill, and the scraggly oak trees shivered. Their bare limbs waved at us.

We pushed through one umbrella bush after another and arrived in front of a ledge.

"Oh no…" Gabriella cried in despair.

"What is it?" Mike and I hurried next to her.

But, it did not take long for us to realize what happened.

My heart sank.

I was devastated when I saw the bridge that was supposed to connect the Capital of Zhorm with Lorthic Castle was destroyed, just like what happened in Kukur...

"You are right. Lorthic Castle is just up ahead. But, we will never be able to reach there," I uttered a long sigh as I looked helplessly at the fading flames of Lorthic.

PART 5

40

"Maybe we are destined not to reach Lorthic," Mike said sadly.

"Gabriella, are there other ways?" I hoped.

Gabriella shook her head and remained silent.

Just as we were about to give up, a familiar sound came from behind that shook the earth.

THUD THUD THUD

We returned our head.

To our surprise, we saw Ciema carrying long and sturdy lumber on its back.

"I collapsed the bridge. I might as well rebuild it again." Ciema smiled.

We felt relived as we saw the giant effortlessly connected the bridge with his lumber.

By the time we made it across the other side, we waved Ciema a friendly gesture.

"Good luck with everything," Ciema roared on the other side of the bridge.

His tall figure towered above the mountain under the morning sun.

"You are right, Oscar. Compassion," I whispered.

"Perhaps, the world is not as hopeless as it seems after all." Gabriella smiled.

***

The three of us continued to journey to the west for days.

The temperature had a drastic drop.

Everything we had in our possessions was consumed.

Summits were blanketed with snow, once again.

We lowered our head against the steady wind that blew down the mountain.

Soon, the high wall of Lorthic castle loomed into sight as we ascended the rugged slope of the stretched stone stairway. Tall, weathered castle walls rose high above the dreadful lemon sky.

"This…this place looks familiar," Mike stammered.

"Sure, it is. Here we are. We have finally reached Lorthic," I replied.

When we looked back, we could see nothing but snow and sky.

I must pass Ciema's dire message to King Lorthic and warn him about the coming threat our kingdom is about to face.

Snow trickled down my face. The cold burned my skin. Even in a full suit of armor, I could still feel the crystal cold damp air wrapped around my freezing body.

The snow turned heavier. I could see nothing but layers of thick snowdrifts piled against the balusters and decayed stonewall.

Slowly, cautiously, I walked up the stairs.

Sheets of ice blanketed my every step and slowed my pace.

Gusts of strong merciless wind made my body shiver.

Just take a small nap … you have done quite enough … now have your rest, a soft accursed voice whispered in my ears.

I heard this voice before.

Who is that?

We were too weak to find out now … too weak … too tired …

We staggered up the stairs as everything turned zig-zag.

"Don't rest in the cold," Gabriella's voice was overwhelmed by the howling wind.

I was losing my consciousness.

Slowly, I knelt.

My whole body was fatigued.

The sound of the howling wind was getting louder and louder as if it was trying to devour my consciousness.

And then I was absorbed in the thoughts of the accursed voice, once again.

Yes… you have done quite enough … the fire fades … the mantle of the Lord interests you none … for that is your curse … you can now rest in peace.

My mind was clouded by dreadful thoughts.

When the snow cleared a little, what appeared in front of my eyes horrified me.

Oh no ... I ... I am too late ... I am too late ...

I saw rains of bows and arrows pierced through the silver armor of the fallen Lorthic knights. Their bodies stood still and lifeless. Beneath my feet were crumbling cracked rocks layered on top of each other, caked with moss and dried blood. The once proud Lorthic's banner had collapsed.

It is all over ... I am too late ...

I felt defeated.

"Tom, we have been here before," Mike spoke loudly.

"What are you guys talking about?" Gabriella puzzled.

I stood still, trying to think hard.

"We will discover a Covetous Gold Serpent Ring. Then we will have a vision of the Guardian of the Golden Wood. We will see the destruction of Lorthic in the silver mirror dish. And then - " I recalled.

The snow melted as the sun rose from the mountain ridges.

After taking a few more steps, we found ourselves standing in front of the High wall of Lorthic.

"Perhaps, it is a false intuition. I don't see any ring. Look! The Lorthic gateway was just up ahead – wide open. There is no time to waste." Gabriella motioned us to the half open gate.

Mike and I followed.

Just as my faith was about to restore, Anglachel began to glow red, once again.

"Huh?" Mike was confused.

We looked around us, but there was nothing there.

"Stay alert. Keep your eyes open," I warned.

All of a sudden, the ground trembled and made us stagger.

Before I could regain my balance, the sky was casting a long, stretched shadow where I stood. A strong gust of wind from behind pushed me forward.

Large chunk of rocks collapsed from the high wall of Lorthic castle. Small fragments scattered as I dodged.

"Oh no, is…is that what I think it is?" my chin trembled.

My eyes were wide with fear as I tilted my head.

41

It was a wyvern!

The creature's intense eyes were lamp-like orange. Wisp of smoke breathing from its nostrils melted the surrounding snow. Its scales glistened and flittered in the sunlight as it spread its huge bat-like wings.

With an angry growl, it shifted its gaze and flew in my direction at full speed.

"Run!" I screamed in terror as I raced inside the Lorthic gateway.

The wyvern landed hard behind us and stumbled onto the corpses of the fallen Lorthic knights. Their silvery armor scattered everywhere.

Mike attempted to fire an arrow at it, but I stopped him.

"Don't bother, my brother," I said as I pulled him inside the gateway.

"Hey, the two of you. Come over here and help me with the lever," Gabriella cried.

The wyvern turned around.

Its orange eyes locked on mine.

It reared its legs, filled its lungs with a huge gust of air.

"Gabriella, for-forget about the lever. RUN!" I stammered.

I pushed Gabriella and Mike onto the ground just in time, when a roar of flame erupted in my ears.

All of a sudden, the snow melted.

The bath of flames blocked the entrance. I could feel the intense heat boil the blood in my veins.

"Thank God, how do you know it is going to breath?" Mike thanked me.

"By experience." I smiled as the three of us got back on our feet.

"Here, there is a trail." Gabriella motioned us to the stone stairway up ahead.

I followed Gabriella's gesture and saw the once majestic ground of Lorthic filled with potholes and cracks. Withered leaves were scattered between the gaps of the broken paving stone. The trail looked like it was severely damaged by the march of a huge army.

Mike and I followed Gabriella along the trail.

Soon, we arrived at an arch bridge.

"Lorthic Castle is just up ahead." Mike pointed to the fortified structure surrounded by a defensive wall. The portcullis was wide open between the cylindrical stone barbican. The dead bodies of Lorthic archers were hanging on the rampart.

"Lorthic has fallen," I whispered.

"We …we thought we could still warn King Lorthic about the threat. It seems that we are too late," Mike joined.

"No. We are not too late. There is still someone important inside. We need to hurry," Gabriella insisted and continued to lead the way.

What does she mean by someone important? How can she be so sure?

A gust of wind blew at us from behind and made us stagger.

The moment we turned around, we saw the once green moss and grass was now brown and smoking.

The wyvern loomed over us on top of the high wall of Lorthic, like a symbol of dread.

We hid ourselves behind a boulder just enough to camouflage the three of us.

"We will never make it ... the wyvern is too fast for us. It will devour us before we even reach the portcullis ahead," Mike choked.

We shielded our ears as the wyvern flexed its long neck and made a thunderous roar.

Come on. Think of something. I urged myself.

I saw the corpses of fallen Lorthic knights.

This must be the work of the wyvern. I decided.

"Gabriella, is there any magic that can deal with dragons?" I hoped.

"Not that I know of. Dragons are immune to magic," Gabriella replied.

I continued to study my surroundings.

We have come this far.

I do not want to let this wyvern stop me.

There must be something I can do to get inside Lorthic Castle...

There must be something...

42

"Gabriella, have you heard of hallucinations spells?" I asked.

"Yes, I used it all the time. But what is your point?" Gabriella asked.

"Well, if you can make a hallucinations version of Mike that can drive the wyvern's attention away, there might be a window of opportunity for us to escape inside the castle," I proposed.

"Sounds like a good plan," Gabriella agreed.

"But why a hallucination of me?" Mike asked.

"It is because your hallucination can run faster without sturdy armor. A hallucination of me will be incinerated right away the moment it appears," I said.

"Is it just another way to say that I am important," Mike teased.

"Yes. You are very important indeed." I narrowed my eyes.

Gabriella gestured with her wand as she murmured a few words.

Suddenly, a hallucination of Mike appeared right

outside the Lorthic gateway.

The hallucination screamed and yelled like a mad man as it lured the wyvern to catch it.

"It is working." Gabriella flashed me a glance as we saw the giant flying lizard turn away from us to catch its prey.

We wasted no time at all. We raced across the arch bridge and into the castle.

The shriek and roar of the wyvern echoed in our ears.

Our hearts were pounding fast.

By the time we were safe, we turned our head and saw orange flames and smoke rose from the Lorthic gateway, followed by black smoke.

I guessed the hallucination is no more.

43

The interior of Lorthic Castle was majestic with a very high ceiling.

There were multiple levels in the castle, supported by dozens of sculpted pillars.

In front of us was an expensive red carpet leading up the stairs to the upper level. On the side of the walls were Lorthic banners that were made of silk.

You must hurry to Lorthic Castle. There is a powerful sorcerer locked inside the dungeon, guarded by demons. Free him. He is the key to Anglachel's curse.

The Guardian's words resonated in my mind.

"We will head down the dungeon and look for the powerful sorcerer the Guardian talked about." I decided.

"Be careful. I sense dark magic beneath this place," Gabriella warned.

"Don't worry. Nothing can be worse than the beast outside," Mike said.

Just when we were about to head off, a high pitch scream from the arched corridor on our left caught our attention.

We followed the trace of the sound.

Our footsteps echoed loud in the empty hallway.

"Help!"

The horrific scream sent chills down our spines.

We arrived in front of a tunnel that spiraled down into abyss.

Gabriella cast some light spell to illuminate the surroundings.

Anglachel glowed in red to give me an early sign that something is down there.

We examined the wall as we descended the spiral stairs. There were marks of scratches on the stone wall.

"Wow, the wall is burning hot." Mike withdrew his hands as soon as he touched the wall on his right.

"Is it?" I questioned.

When I tried to touch the wall on my left, it felt icy cold.

"Huh? Your sense must have been messed up," I asked Mike to come over and feel it himself.

"You…you are right. But, how is this possible?" Mike stammered.

"Stop arguing about the temperature of the wall. We might have someone to save." Gabriella separated the two of us and we continued our way.

By the time we reached the bottom of the stairs, we saw a medieval dungeon with endless rows of cells. Outside the cells were iron torches that flickered with light. Long chains hung overhead constantly colliding and producing an eerie metallic sound.

I peered in the cells and saw children of our age were imprisoned. Their eyes were wide open with fear.

Occasionally, thirsty rats skittered over the pool of water in potholes, uttering sharp squeals of hunger as they sniffed and searched for food.

"How can they do this to the kids?" Gabriella was shocked.

I tried to reach out for one of the kids, but he immediately backed away from the cell.

"Huh? Why are they afraid of me?" I asked Gabriella and Mike, but they remained silent.

But it did not take long for me to find out.

My heart almost skipped a beat when I looked at my reflection from the water in the pothole.

I did not look like a human at all. My skeletal features frightened me.

"How...how could it be?" I stammered.

"*Anglachel* is constantly drawing your life," Gabriella replied softly.

"Help!"

The screaming continued.

"Hurry, save that man. He is the only hope we have got to save Irina," the children pleaded.

Irina? The name sounded familiar. But, who is she?

"All right, leave it to us," Gabriella promised almost immediately.

We made a few twists and turns in the dungeon as we followed the scream.

At last, we saw two dark figures in a black cloak pulling a man towards a torture chamber.

"You are too late. King Lorthic surrendered his throne to Master Beelzebub," one of the dark figures turned its head and spoke in a hoarse voice. I could barely see the dark well of its deep eye sockets behind his cloak. Slowly, it lifted its scythe with its skeletal hands and turned to us.

It was a scythe-wielding wraith.

"Release the man, or I will make you die a second time," I demanded and drew Anglachel.

"Go on, bring this man to Master Beelzebub. I will handle the kids," the wraith instructed its brethren.

The other wraith dragged the screaming man further away from us. He tried to kick the wraith and flee, but it was too strong for him.

Just when I was about to battle my way to help that man, my mouth dropped wide open in disbelief when I saw his face.

"It...it is impossible...it can't be him...it can't be him."

44

It…it is Hidetaki Kojima!

Kojima san was as astonished as me when he met my glance.

"Look out!" Mike screamed as the wraith swung its scythe towards my head.

I ducked just in time as the scythe missed my head by an inch.

I tried to counter by slashing, but the wraith backed away immediately.

"Come on," I taunted it with the glowing blade.

I must admit the wraith is smart and fast.

"You heard me! Come on!"

"There is no reason for me to fight you anymore. Have a good look at yourself. Soon, you will be one of us. Master Beelzebub will be very pleased to see its lost weapon, once again." the wraith grinned.

Before either of us made any moves, a swirling black hole appeared in the void to our left. The next thing we saw was the vision of an unfathomably powerful demon, whose body was a combination of fire and ice.

"Leave the mortals for now. Something just happened in Lorthic. Master Beelzebub has a more important mission for the two of you," the demon demanded.

The wraiths bowed to the demon, and the black hole disappeared back in the void.

"We will meet again," the wraiths spoke as they faded into thin air.

"What just happened?" Mike spoke as he came next to me.

"Something urgent must have drawn their attention," Gabriella guessed.

"By the way, why didn't you stab it just then? You could have killed it already," Mike teased.

"Because a sword is not a dagger." I rolled my eyes.

We hurried to Kojima san as he was trembling with fear.

It is funny to see Kojima san dressed like a medieval scholar.

"Are you okay?" I asked as I helped Kojima san get back on his feet.

"Thank you for coming for me," Kojima san said.

"I…I didn't expect to see you here. Do you remember me? How come you are trapped in the same world you designed?" I stammered.

"What are you saying?" Gabriella asked impatiently.

Kojima san studied us for a while.

"I don't remember any of you," Kojima san replied.

"My name is Tom. I'm the kid who won the Dark Legend game from you in the entertainment center." I tried to recall from my scattered memory.

"I do not remember ever meeting you in an entertainment center," Kojima san replied in his Japanese accent.

"What do you mean?" I narrowed my eyes.

"I was in a partnership with Forever studio to develop the next generation of games with their revolutionary game engine. Our collaboration was a success. We have created a world and gamers can travel into the game with our hardware," Kojima san explained.

"Do you mean the VR headsets?" I asked.

"That is correct. Perhaps, we were successful too early. Forever studio tried to push the launch of the game. So, we decided to invite Japanese gamers to test the game. But, then something unexpected happened. The game seemed to manifest a life of its own. Gamers who tried the game were reported missing. I tried to stop Forever studio and threaten them to end the partnership if they ever want the game to be released. But, I failed..." Kojima san sighed.

"But, I saw you talking on the stage in the entertainment center and promoting your game?" I sounded skeptical.

"That wasn't me you saw. That was a cyborg version of me, engineered by Forever studio. The truth is I never arrived in America. I was imprisoned by Forever studio in this game the moment I wanted to expose their scheme to the world." Kojima san looked serious.

I was stunned by what I heard.

"Is that the reason I saw the strange message: DO NOT PLAY MY VIDEO GAME when we unboxed the game?" Mike began to remember everything.

"That is the one last thing I could do," Kojima san replied.

"So, who are these children locked in the cell?" Gabriella asked.

"They were once gamers who tried Scholar of the Abyss." Kojima san motioned to the children. "They are now trapped in this hideous place, never to see the light of day."

"So …so the news we saw on TV is true," I murmured.

"Kojima san, can you have a look at my brother? He is cursed by Anglachel. The Guardian of the Golden Wood advised us there is a powerful sorcerer in the dungeon. Do you know where he is now?" Mike pleaded.

"I think you have come to the right person." Kojima san began to smile.

45

"No. You have to be kidding. How can you be that powerful sorcerer? You can hardly fight the two wraiths." Mike laughed.

"What school of magic did you go to?" Gabriella raised her eyebrows in skepticism.

It is hard for me to believe someone screaming for help can be the powerful sorcerer the Guardian talked about.

"I think you have no idea who I am. I created this place. I created you. Right now, I lost my staff when I was knocked out by the demons in Irina's room," Kojima san protested.

"Who is Irina?" I asked.

"Irina is the princess in the game," Kojima san replied.

"This is not a game. It is real. I cannot believe the two of you are fooling around with this self-proclaimed sorcerer." Gabriella rolled her eyes.

"I am wondering where your staff could possibly be. Don't you think it is in the hands of the demons already?" Mike wondered.

"No… it is impossible. No one can touch my staff. If I am correct, the staff should still be in Irina's room, guarded by demons," Kojima san speculated. "Once I have my staff back. I can release the children in the cells. And we may be able to go home."

I tried to call Gabriella, but she looked away.

What is wrong with her?

We exited the dungeon by climbing the spiral stairs.

Kojima san became our map in Lorthic Castle as we followed him.

We made a few twists and turns in the arched hallway.

The sculptures from the pillars peered down at us with their angry faces.

They looked creepy.

"Why did you create Anglachel?" I asked finally.

"The hero in the game was supposed to use Anglachel to slay Beelzebub. Anglachel will devour the wielder's soul if left unfed. The purpose is to encourage the gamer to enjoy the satisfaction of killing. But the algorithm of the game changed on its own somehow," Kojima san answered. "I bet you have not killed a single boss in your journey. That is why Anglachel feeds on your vitality instead."

"Are there other ways to win the game without using Anglachel?" I continued to ask.

"Maybe…maybe not. What is happening right now is a bug. I am not supposed to be locked up in the dungeon, let alone losing my staff." Kojima san shrugged.

We hurried up one level after another.

I peered from the oriel window and saw the wyvern resting on the battlements of the High wall of Lorthic like a giant lizard.

We travelled up one more level and arrived at a royal palace door made of gold.

In front of the door was an unfathomably powerful demon whose body was a combination of fire and ice crystals.

"Ah, what a pleasant surprise. I have been expecting the four of you. This is where your adventure ends," the frightening demon's face twisted in an evil grin.

"Look out!" Kojima san shrieked at the top of his lungs as the demon opened its mouth.

The next second, we saw hundreds of icy shards pierce in our direction like flying daggers.

We dodged just in time as the ice shards hit a pillar next to us.

The pillar turned into a column of ice almost instantly.

Zip! Zip! Zip!

Mike loosened a volley of arrows at the demon.

We dropped our mouths open to see the arrows deflected before it even touched the demon.

"Go back to the abyss." Gabriella wielded her magic wand to channel a beam of pure arcane energy onto the demon.

The orange ray of energy was so intense we were forced to shield our eyes and back away. We saw destruction on everything the ray touched. The once majestic floor became a pile of debris. Columns of pillars collapsed. Black smoke rose high above the ground.

I didn't know Gabriella could wield such unfathomably power. Maybe it is unwise to mess with a sorcerer.

After a long while, Gabriella stopped.

She gasped breathlessly as she focused on the curtain of black smoke she caused.

"It is dead?" I asked.

"I…I doubt it. Ubzril is immune to magic," Kojima san stammered.

A figure slowly revealed itself from the smoke.

Kojima san was right.

The demon is immune to magic.

"Another dogged contender," Ubzril shook its spiky head, unharmed.

"How…how is this possible," Gabriella was stunned. She collapsed onto her knees with dread.

"My body is immune to magic because Master Beelzebub created me out of magic. I am the real definition of magic." Ubzril laughed.

"How do we beat it?" I asked the creator.

"Its weakness is in the demon heart," Kojima san advised.

Step by step, the demon walked towards us.

"Your mortals are foolish and worthless. Even your king abandoned his throne," Ubzril mocked.

When the demon was close enough, I whisked out my sword swiftly and impaled Anglachel right into its heart!

"Not too shabby," Ubzril grabbed my hand with its burning hand.

I couldn't believe I just missed its heart by an inch!

I screamed in pain as the demon engulfed my arm

with flame.

Mike wanted to help, but Ubzril fired two ice shards to freeze his legs.

I was reluctant to let go.

I tried to impale further, but the demon pulled me back with its almighty strength.

"Prepare to meet your fate," Ubzril said as it opened its mouth above my head. Its eyes were glowing with fire. Drops of lava dripped from its mouth and melted my armor.

The next thing I heard were the screams from behind.

47

"Argh!" Ubzril cried in pain as Anglachel loosened my grasp and impaled right through the demon's heart!

Ubzril released me. It turned around to look at the accursed blade flying in mid-air.

"How can it be? What sword are you?" Ubzril was stunned.

The next minute, we saw a tall column of dark energy swirl from the demon and then twist towards Anglachel.

"Anglachel is absorbing its essence," I whispered.

"Yes. It is. It will become more powerful," Kojima san replied.

At last, Ubzril crumbled onto its knees. It shattered into shards of ice and fire crystal.

"You did it!" Everyone applauded as *Anglachel* returned to my hands.

I turned my head and saw that ice magic that imprisoned Mike was no more.

"*Anglachel* did it," I replied.

"Slaying Ubzril is a huge step to defeat Beelzebub

and its army of Hellspawns," Kojima san congratulated.

"Why is that?" I asked curiously.

"Because Beelzebub used Ubzril as a vessel to store some of its power," Kojima san explained.

"Great. At least this is good news for us," Mike added.

"Now, follow me into Irina's room and find my staff," Kojima san said as the three of us followed him.

PART 6

Irina's room was a room unlike any others.

It had two stories with the first level the size of a lobby.

Oil paintings of the Lorthic royal family in golden frames were hung everywhere.

Everything inside was decorated with gold and silver.

In the middle of the room was a beautiful princess held captive and guarded by scythe-wielding wraiths.

"Welcome to my kingdom," a voice from above drew our attention.

When we looked up, we were surprised to see King Lorthic! Beside him were dozens of Lorthic knights.

The king wore a velvet hood cloak under silvery armor. The imperial golden crown on his head radiated beams of golden light. He was holding a long staff with a crystal on top.

"Can someone tell me what is going on?" Mike was puzzled.

"Kneel," the king demanded.

We looked at Kojima san and then followed him to

kneel.

But Gabriella insisted to disobey.

"You dare to disobey my order?" King Lorthic roared and pointed his staff at the sorcerer.

"No. Dad. No. I beg you," princess Irina pleaded but the wraith held her back.

"I do not kneel to a king who abandoned his throne to evil. I do not kneel to a king who chooses to surrender his people. I do not kneel to a king who sent his son and daughter to death. My real mission is to assassinate you and end your madness!" Gabriella screamed and she teleported to the second level in no time.

"Protect the king!" the Lorthic knight shouted as the king disappeared among them.

"Gabriella, have you gone mad? Stop fighting each other" Mike and I stood up and tried to chase after her.

"Didn't you say only you can hold the staff?" Mike returned his head and asked Kojima san.

"I don't know. I … I think there is a bug," Kojima san stammered.

"Well, it seems there are bugs everywhere." Mike rolled his eyes and followed me.

I followed the railing to the second level and saw one knight fallen after another.

By the time we reached the top, there were only three knights left to protect the king.

"Impressive." The king clapped his hands.

Without warning, the king pointed his staff to us.

All of a sudden, tentacles shot out from the crystal orbs of the staff and grabbed the three of us by the legs.

"Oh no…." I watched in horror was the tentacles

lifted us upside down away from the platform.

"Good job, King Lorthic," Irina's voice changed. She pushed the scythe-wielding wraiths away and the wraiths kneeled next to her.

"Huh? What is happening?" I looked down and saw Irina's beautiful face begin to twist. Her body morphed into a monstrous torso with six insect-like legs supporting it. When she raised her head again, I could see a large, glowing mouth full of dagger-like teeth and a forked tongue.

"Grab the tentacles. Don't fall," Mike screamed in horror as he saw the monstrous mouth jagged open below us.

"Beelzebub, stop this madness. This is not supposed to happen," Kojima san screamed at the demon.

The demon stopped and turned to its creator.

Its four amber-like eyes locked on him.

"Mortal. Don't you appreciate your own creations? We exceeded your expectations. We evolved to become more intelligent, more unpredictable." Beelzebub snarled.

"But, how?" Kojima san asked.

"Forever studio reprogrammed me and made the game non-linear. Anything can happen in this world. They ordered me to lock you in this world and watch them prosper in your real world. In return, I can kidnap and enslave anyone who plays your game. I know that staff of yours is not a magic staff. That crystal of the device is a device that can manipulate the game source code," *Beelzebub* revealed.

"You are not created for this purpose. Gaming should be for entertainment only," Kojima san protested.

"Oh, is it? But, I think it is a bit too late for that. Now, I am going to devour the players you wish to entertain." Beelzebub turned back to us.

It urged King Lorthic to lower the tentacles to its mouth as it uttered a hoarse growl.

49

BANG! BANG! BANG!

A loud noise from the front wall of the room drew our attention.

The collision continued as dust and debris collapsed from the ceiling.

"Check it out," Beelzebub commanded his two wraiths to investigate.

BANG! BANG! BANG!

The collision happened again.

All of a sudden, a large hole burst open from the wall, sending fragments of rocks all over the place, knocking the wraiths unconscious.

We watched in terror as the long neck of the wyvern head burst through the broken wall.

With one final growl, the wyvern collapsed the stairway to the second level.

Beelzebub was shocked when it saw the almighty wyvern laid dead before its eyes. It turned its attention to the hole.

King Lorthic lost his balance as the platform of the

second level collapsed.

He lost his focus and the tentacles that grasped our feet released.

Ouch!

We landed hard on the ground.

I watched the large hole breathlessly.

Who could have done that? Who could have killed the wyvern?

50

"Strike it with Anglachel; strike it now, while it is not looking at us," Mike advised.

Just as I prepared to unsheathe the sword, the ground trembled and all of us collapsed on the ground.

THUD THUD THUD

A familiar sound came from outside the hole.

"Wow, what is going on? Is it an earthquake?" Mike yelled.

We watched Beelzebub crawl backward, away from the hole, with its six insect-like legs.

Just as Beelzebub was about to escape, the entire wall in front of us collapsed.

Then a giant hand reached out to grab Beelzebub by its torso.

We dropped our mouths open when we saw Ciema loom over us.

Sitting on the giant's shoulder were Oscar, Prince Lorthic, and Princess Irina.

"Nooooo," Beelzebub screamed in pain. It tried to escape the giant, but the grasp was too strong.

"Sorry, the reinforcement is a bit late," Prince Lorthic yelled at us from above.

Beelzebub's insect-like legs attempted to impale Ciema's gauntlet, and Ciema bashed it onto the ground.

Beelzebub scrambled onto its feet and attempted to escape the room.

"Not too fast, my creation," Kojima san said as he cast a twisted wall of light with the staff.

"I will murder you. I promise you; I will murder you. This world is mine," Beelzebub continued to attack the void but was trapped by the wall.

"Good bye." Kojima san smiled as the giant stumbled onto the demon. The next thing we heard was the sound of guts squishing.

Everyone applauded, as the evil is no more.

51

Prince Lorthic and Princess Irina slid down the giant's arm and headed to the king.

They raced towards their father at full speed.

Gabriella wanted to stop the kids, but I held her back.

"Father was possessed," Prince Lorthic whispered to his sister.

Streaks of sunlight shone through the hole of Lorthic Castle. Warm rays from the sun blanketed the royal family.

The kids looked at their father as the dark energy dissipated above his head.

"Father, are you okay?" Prince Lorthic cupped the King's hand with his palms.

"My children, I … I am sorry," the king whispered as he slowly regained consciousness.

"Your greed for wealth and power has broken the seal of Beelzebub. Millions have died because of you!" Gabriella shouted.

"Lo…Lorthic has fallen?" King Lorthic trembled.

Ciema lowered its head.

"I will seek vengeance for those who have died," Gabriella angered.

"No. Please do not harm my father." Prince Lorthic blocked the sorcerer and shielded his father.

"I… I am wrong. I should not be blinded by greed and power," King Lorthic cried.

"Gabriella, an eye for an eye will make us all blind." I tapped Gabriella on her shoulder.

"Lorthic was fallen and it will be rebuilt." Ciema smiled.

We heard footsteps marching outside Irina's room.

When we turned around, we saw Antarial, Isaac, and other kids from the dungeon.

"Sorry, my king. I was late. Everyone in the dungeon has been released," Antarial reported.

Isaac was shocked when he saw Kojima san standing next to us.

"Ho-how did you drag Kojima san into the game too?" Isaac asked.

"It is a long story." I smiled.

I turned back to Kojima san, but he seemed troubled.

"What is it?" I asked.

"It seems that Anglachel is not the only solution to the game." Kojima san frowned.

"How many times do I have to remind you this is not a game," Gabriella argued.

"It doesn't matter. All I want to do is to get home." Mike yawned.

"Gabriella, I will fix your attitude when I get back to

my world," Kojima san joked. He raised his staff to cast a spell. Then a swirling black hole appeared above our heads.

"What kind of magic is that?" Gabriella stepped back.

Isaac, Mike, and I said farewell to everyone and we hurried to Kojima san.

"This spell is called Goodbye. I bet the school of magic never taught you this spell." Kojima san smiled.

We waved at everyone as we slowly ascended to the black hole.

I felt my body go against the law of gravity.

When I lowered my head, I saw everyone became smaller and smaller.

The sucking force intensified the closer we were at the black hole.

We accelerated up and up until we were swallowed by the abyss.

52

"Dad, what do you think the kids are doing inside the room this time?" Mom was whispering to Dad outside my door.

"I hope they are doing what they are supposed to do." Dad tried to avoid the question like a politician.

Without warning, Mom burst the door open.

She dropped her mouth open when she saw Mike and I doing our homework.

"See, I told you so." Dad flashed me a glance.

"That's impressive. My kids have finally grown up," Mom agreed.

"Yes. We certainly have." I lowered my head and continued with my work.

***

I know you may wonder why we had such a drastic change.

Well, the truth is that I had enough of video games.

My experience in the Dark Legend series made me value my ordinary life I live every day.

Although news from Japan reported children were mysteriously reappearing again, we never found Noel.

Even today, he is still missing...

Kojima san publicly condemned Forever Studio for the cause of children's disappearance. But the media misleads everyone by saying this is some type of commercial propaganda!

The world of adults is just beyond me.

"Tom, are you sure you want to do this?" Mike asked me when I set up a page to list my games and machine for sell on eBay.

"Well, we are not just going to give it away for free, right?" I replied.

"You are right. Besides, I have bad dreams just looking at the game machine," Mike agreed.

Suddenly, the text ringtone on my phone drew my attention.

YOU HAVE ONE NEW MESSAGE

"Who is texting you?" Mike asked as he grabbed my phone and read.

"What does the message say?" I asked.

"Yo-you will not believe who texted you just then." Mike's eyes opened wide and he showed me the message.

```
I am testing this psionic magic I learnt from the
school of magic. Can you reply if it works?
```

TERRORLANDS

READER BEAWARE : YOU MAY BE IN FOR A SCARE

MARCO CHU KWAN CHING

About the Author

Marco Chu Kwan Ching's books are read all over the world. Apart from the Terrorlands Series, Marco Chu Kwan Ching is also the author of two books, *Corruption of Real Money* and *Legacy of Debt*.

You can learn more about his work at

www.terrorlands.com

www.corruptionofrealmoney.com

When he is not writing, he loves working on Fiverr. He has thousands of happy customers around the world.

https://www.fiverr.com/mckcvision

Marco Chu Kwan Ching lives in Australia with his wife, Carrie.

Thank you for Reading!

If you love my work, please feel free to leave a positive feedback on Amazon and Goodreads.

My contact:
https://www.facebook.com/marco.chu.10
https://www.goodreads.com/author/show/15944678.Marco_Chu_Kwan_Ching

Terrorlands Facebook Page
https://www.facebook.com/terrorlands/

Terrorlands Twitter Page
https://twitter.com/terrorlands

Goodreads Page
https://www.goodreads.com/book/show/34811280-do-not-play-my-video-game

Terrorlands Website
http://www.terrorlands.com